The Crystal Heart

Beginnings

Arctic Flame Publications
Port Orchard, Washington

The Crystal Heart: Beginnings
Copyright 2013 by Anthony M. Swinsinski
Published by Arctic Flame Publications
Author Photo by Kyla Deisler Photography
Trade Paperback Edition
November 5, 2013
ISBN: 0615916562
ISBN-13: 978-0615916569

For information about film, reprint or other subsidiary rights, contact: AFPRights@gmail.com

Specializing in imaginative ebook and print books, Arctic Flame Publications works exclusively with authors who do not want to adhere to the current trends in the industry.

Arctic Flame Publications
www.ArcticFlamePublications.com
www.facebook.com/ArcticFlamePublications
AFPRights@gmail.com

To my own Kinley, wherever you are, if I have met you or not, you are the main character in this book as you are in my life, thank you for repairing my own, very real, Crystal Heart. Take care of it.

To my friends and family, those who have given me advice and helped throughout the long process of writing this book, to those who have inspired characters in this book, both the good and the bad; you have entered and/or exited my life for a reason.

Thank you, you made this possible.

Finally, yet importantly, the individuals.

Bridgett Swinsinski, always there and egging me on to keep writing.

Penny Swinsinski, My dog, always by my side while I'm writing.

Table of Contents

PRONUNCIATION GUIDE

Aislin ……………………………. ASH-lin
Arathia …………………….. uh-rey-thee-uh
Arathian ……………………….. uh-rey-thee-in
Arissa ………………………… uh-RISS-ah
Caedmon …………………..… KAD-mon
Enat ……………………...………... AY-net
Esras ……………………...………… ESS rass
Fallyn ……..………………………….. FAL-un
Illumistration …….. i-loo-muh-strey-shuh n
Innogen …………………………. In-oh-jen
Keeva …………………….………… kee-vah
Kieron ………………………….... KEER an
Kinley …………………………… KIN-lee
Peadar …………………………… PAD ar
Ree-Kyae …………………...…… Ree-k yā
Varian ………….………………. vair-ee-in

The Crystal Heart

Heart

Beginnings

Prologue

The Crystal Heart

It was dark, as always, the old men gathered around the fire again. The wind picked up and sparks swirled above the flames that were gently licking the logs. One of the men in the circle began to speak; his old and wise voice began to weave a tale as he reached into a woven pouch tied around his waste, pulling from it, a handful of golden dust. He threw the dust onto the flames, turning them purple, then they changed to a dark blue, and finally they were almost as black as the darkness that surrounded everything. The fire was waiting for him, patiently waiting to show his story to those who were gathered around, and, as he spoke, shapes began to form in the flames. They started dancing together, intertwining with the words of his story and illustrating it from a blurry perspective.

The Crystal Heart: Beginnings

"It's been a long time since we have seen real light. Not firelight, not glow-grub light, but real light. Our land is barren now, it was once lush and green, animals roamed the hills and our hunting was plentiful. That was before we knew to protect it, before we knew The Crystal Heart could even be broken."

A heart appeared in the flames, refracting light around the surrounding area. Rainbows were dancing off the men who were sitting around the fire as the heart gently turned, suspended in midair. It was flawless, perfectly cut and it looked so solid that one of the men tried reaching into the inferno to pull it out, as if to rescue it from the burning flames, now licking around it. He withdrew his hands and they were red and blistered. Ignoring the interruption, the wise old storyteller began speaking again.

"Legend has it that The Crystal Heart was given to us by our god. He was a beautiful man, and he loved us more than anyone could ever love anybody."

A perfectly sculpted face appeared in the flames. The most dominant feature on the face were his sad eyes, they almost hid his lips, and they definitely outshone the dark curly hair that reached half way down his forehead. With each storyteller, the man looked different; the illumistration was what the storyteller saw in his mind's eye, projected through the fire.

"Our world was dark and we were barely surviving, he didn't want to see us parish so he ripped open his chest and pulled out his own heart. With the rest of his strength he climbed the highest mountain and placed his heart on top so that its light would shine forever, this was the light of his love. He wanted it to reach out to every corner of the land. He was bleeding badly from the deep and crudely torn skin and tissue of his chest and everywhere that his blood touched something grew; trees, plants, and animals sprang from dust and air with his blood as the fuel for life."

The fire showed the story as he spoke. It showed the well-built man with only one hand free, making his way up a craggy mountain, clutched in his free hand was the brightest part of the fire, The Crystal Heart. The light coming from The Crystal Heart seemed to pulsate, growing brighter and dimming in a hypnotic rhythm. The man continued to bleed from his chest and red fire poured out.

Wherever the red fire drenched a piece of the brown mountain, new life sprang forth. There were animals never before seen in Arathia, creatures with eyes the size of fruit, and as tall as trees walked around on four legs. Birds of every shape and color exploded from the side of the mountain and took to the air. As the blood rolled down the mountain, it spread over every inch of ground and into the rivers and over the other side. Trees in shapes never known sprung up from the now rolling green hills and plants, with vines that spread across the dirt seemed to grow in fast forward, they were blurred and out of focus as if being seen through tear soaked eyes.

"When the heart was placed on the mountain the man dissipated, the golden dust that his body turned into was blown in every direction by the wind; it was sucked up into the sky, and pulled down into the darkest depths of the water. We still breathe him in today."

At this point the man paused from telling his story and inhaled deeply, the light from the fire accented the shadows of his face and made him look even older than he was. He reached into the woven pouch and lifted another handful of the golden dust; he held his hand to his face and opened it. The golden dust seemed to flow over his hand as if it were smoke; he released his breath slowly and the golden dust poured onto the fire; and the flames roared to life. The fire exploded into a brilliant white-yellow light as golden sparks danced with each other and flew in all directions; they floated up and dissolved into the air. He smiled and continued telling his story.

"Unlike us, the Ree-Kyae flourished in the darkness. Those disgusting and hateful beings thrived until The Crystal Heart was placed on the mountain, and they had no Man-God to bring the darkness back to them. They retreated into caves deep underground. They were jealous of the love that the Man-God showed for us, it ate at them from the inside out. The Ree-Kyae disappeared and we rarely saw them. The light from The Crystal Heart never went out, and the Ree-Kyae couldn't survive in the light. It was pure, it was love, it was everything good and they were a race made of pure evil and hatred. They enjoyed hurting us, torturing us in their dark world. They would kidnap our children for slavery and raid our camps, stealing our food and capturing our best fighters, pitting them against each other in a fight to the death, all for their amusement."

"Once The Crystal Heart was placed on top of the mountain they had no choice but to retreat into caves and tunnels. A lot of them didn't make it to the caves or even the temporary cover of shadow. They clawed their way to the closest form of shelter, the ones that didn't make it provided food for the new animals that had sprung to life from the blood of the Man-God. Those that did make it to the caves built extravagant underground cities, and there they stayed waiting for a time when they could return to the life that they previously knew."

The firelight changed, dulling to a low yellow orange and black silhouettes were crawling toward dark blue hollows in the flames. A close up was shown of a Ree-Kyae face, its teeth were sharp and pointed, it had dark black eyes with no whites to them, and no hair grew atop its pale head. Its nose, if you could call it a nose, was almost nonexistent, merely three vertical slits in the center of its face, its mouth opened and the fire roared.

The fire started crackling, hissing as the skin of the Ree-Kyae started peeling and boiling, as the light from The Crystal Heart touched it. The scene followed this Ree-Kyae, it clutched at the dirt as it tried to drag itself into the mouth of a nearby cave, but the light was expanding fast. The Ree-Kyae fell to the ground; its amazingly dark eyes darkened just a little more as the life left its body. Its hand landed in the shadows of the cave that it was struggling to reach. Another Ree-Kyae was watching and as the hand hit the shadow, it reached down, picked up the lifeless hand and tore off a mouthful of meat from right below the thumb with its sharp teeth. Time passed faster in the fire now, Animals surrounded the bodies of the many fallen Ree -Kyae, gnawing at them until there was nothing left but splinters of bone, too small for the animals to consider.

"The newly born animals feasted on the bodies of the dead, and the wounds left on the survivors by the light of The Crystal Heart never healed, they served as constant reminders to generation after generation of Ree-Kyae. They were passed down from parent to child, establishing well-known families and clans. Their wounds festered, giving life to the scent of death; it follows them everywhere they go. However, the repulsive sores weren't the only new addition to the Ree-Kyae's physical appearance, they started changing, adapting to their new lives."

The fire showed full Ree-Kyae families, fathers, sons, mothers, daughters, and grandparents, all with the same sores in the same pattern. The flame showed minor changes in physical appearance to a few of the generations, the three slits they caught scents from closed gradually, leaving a fleshy patch of skin where they once were. Their eyes grew wider, their ears started to point upwards and their skin radiated with its own light, so dull that the ground below their feet was barely illuminated.

"The Ree-Kyae grew even more hateful and jealous towards us, their sores burned, and they came up with idea after idea to destroy The Crystal Heart. They tried launching stones, sticks, and even various bones from the cave openings, however, their projectiles never managed to land their mark. They tried digging tunnels under it so that it would fall in and they could bury it, but it hovered in the air untouched."

The flames showed various items hurled from cave mouths in the mountains, it seemed that at the last second, the wind would pick up and the piece of refuse drifted to either side. The flame zoomed in on the image of the heart and the ground under it began to tremble. Piece by piece it started collapsing in on itself from the center, a hole opened in the earth, jagged. An arm reached out, it looked as if it had been laden with years of rot and decay. The fingers on the hand came to sharp points as it reached towards the heart; they seemed bent at unnatural and painful angles. The arm blackened, as it got closer to The Crystal Heart, the skin started flaking off, it was turning to ash and the pieces were carried away on the wind. Before the arm was completely gone, it was pulled back into the hole, the owner apparently giving up. The Crystal Heart still hovered in its spot; above the hole in the ground, the light it emanated was still pulsating.

The old man paused and inhaled. He looked around the circle at the faces around him. They were captivated by his stories, he was well known for the detail in his illumistrations. He reached into the woven bag again and willed the fire to hang onto the picture of The Crystal Heart. He felt the dust in his hand, not dry like every other dust, but as more of a wet sensation between his fingers, like sticking his hand in a stream or puddle after it rains. The Crystal Heart hovered and rotated slowly in the fire, in one swift movement, he flung the handful of dust onto the fire and it roared, this was supposed to be the rage of the leader of the Ree-Kyae, the frustration of the many different plans not working. Violently the fire switched between the colors of black and bright red, to yellow then orange.

Angry colors thought the old man, and the fire obeyed, he continued reciting the legend.

"The Crystal Heart was the impenetrable center of our world, the most precious thing on the planet. It sustained the life of the plants, the animals, and it drove down our tormentors, it was eternal, or so we thought. The Ree-Kyae did it; they found a way to destroy The Crystal Heart. It took them an extremely long time, and many different generations tried and failed. The refuse that was hurled at it hadn't even come close to touching it, and obviously The Crystal Heart couldn't fall, because it didn't touch the ground, it was suspended in the air on the mountain, and so it would stay, unless moved elsewhere."

"There was a traitor with us, handsome throughout his life; he had always gotten what he wanted. The women he wanted, the food he wanted, the living spaces he wanted, and he was very upset when he was turned down. She couldn't stand him, but he obsessed over the idea of lying with her. He propositioned her again and again, but each time she told him no. He grew furious, he wanted her, and he always got exactly what he wanted, he snuck into her home, he shoved her to the ground. She hit her head and didn't move, at first he was worried he had killed her, but then he saw her chest, it moved up and down with breath, though only faintly. While she was there, unconscious, he took what he wanted from her."

The fire spat upward, it showed a muscular man with straight black hair cut chin length. It showed him watching a woman through her tent window. Her hair was straight and black and hung down to the small of her back, where his features were angular and rugged hers were delicate and beautifully feminine. Her lips were full and tender, they looked soft, her eyes were a bright blue and her skin was tan. He walked to the front of the tent when her back was turned, and slipped in. The shadows on the tent were all that was visible, you could tell the woman was facing away and he was walking up behind her. First, he grabbed her by the arms and spun her around. His shadow pressed its face to hers and she pushed him away, his arms wrapped tight around her waist, it was clear he had no intention of letting her go. When he was finished kissing her, he threw her to the floor, there was a little hesitation from his shadow as she lay there, he climbed on top of her, and then the scene went dark.

"The council didn't take this matter lightly. The man was brought to them and tortured before having his sentence read aloud. He was to be castrated and banished. Anger flooded his face. He screamed at the council calling the woman a whore, stating that she wasn't worth the trouble, but the council wasn't to be swayed on their decision. Just as their sentence stated would happen, he was castrated and cast out, the mark was tattooed on his forehead."

A group of men were sitting at a circular stone table in the fire, the muscular man was lying on the table bound and stripped naked, there were instruments surrounding him, red liquid fire puddled on the table, dripping down the sides onto the floor. The taut skin that stretched over his muscles were filled with gouges and scratches and many cuts, liquid fire flowed freely from his wounds. In front of each man around the table were different torture devices, Foot Presses, Lead Sprinklers, Thumbscrews and The Heretic's Fork were among many other tools. On the man's forehead was a symbol, it glowed with the most clarity in the scene. There were three wavy, blood red lines that came together at their lower most points, a circle bound them, it was thick at the bottom and almost non-existent at the top, the points of the lines were in its center, and the whole symbol was outlined in black. The woman walked in the room, she had a devious smile on her face as she looked down at the man. Her fist was clenched around the handle of a rusty knife so tightly that her knuckles were white. The fire zoomed in on the man's face and it was plain to see he was in agony, his mouth opened wide in a scream, his pain was allowed no sound by the old storyteller, instead the fire emulated a faint laugh, high pitched, the laugh of a woman.

"The man was thrown out of the village still bound and bleeding, no clothing covering his body. Blood was running down from between his legs, he was given the rusty knife the woman had used to take her vengeance. If he wanted to get out of his ropes, he had to cut himself out somehow. The village that he belonged to packed up their caravans and left as soon as he was out of their hands, they were assuming he would be eaten by animals. He got the bindings off his legs but not from around his ankles and was able to stand up. He hopped over to one of the nearby caves hoping to rub the bindings that were cutting the circulation to his hands on the wall of rough rock, but the Ree-Kyae had been inside, watching as much of the event as they could see. They intercepted him; they started a new plan after the failing of all before. Find someone else who would be able to go into the light and see if they are able to get near enough to The Crystal Heart to destroy it."

There was another roar from the flames as the illumistration of the cave vanished; the fire died down to a smolder, as if it didn't want to go on illustrating the story. The storyteller hadn't planned this, the fires always tried to die at this point, but he was expecting it. He threw a couple fresh logs onto the smoldering coals and covered it with more of the golden dust. It flowed over the logs, pouring down the bark until it reached the smoldering coals. The fire growled and popped in protest as it consumed the wood. The old man started forming the pictures in his mind as he spoke. Urging his friend, the flame, to take what he was thinking and show those around him. The fire listened and, after a short while, accepted.

"The man stumbled to the cave, making sure his skin didn't touch the shadows inside. The light from The Crystal Heart was his only protection. It was common knowledge that the Ree-Kyae couldn't be out of shadows or they would die, but not as common that they didn't die instantaneously. If they chose to deal with the pain of the light and more sores, they can stand it for a few moments. The traitor rubbed his wrists up and down on the rough rock wall."

This is what made the old storyteller so famous, he could show things in the fire that he wasn't saying. The man was rubbing his bound wrists on the cave wall, keeping his balance, but what the storyteller hadn't said, and what the fire showed, was an arm thick with sores emerging from shadows. As it entered the light the flesh boiled and melted away, leaving thick blisters behind. Smoke rose from the fingertips and the skin of the forearm, as it slowly made its way closer to the man's shoulder. His nose wrinkled as if he smelled something disgusting, which he probably had, the scent of death and decay lingered at the mouth of any cave or opening in the ground.

"This Ree-Kyae went through a lot of pain to grab the traitor, but its goal was accomplished." The arm swung across the man and pulled him into the cave; the man tried to struggle but he had lost his footing, and was still bound.

"They spent a long time with the traitor, poisoning his mind even further, poking his injuries, pulling them apart right as they had started to scab to make sure they didn't heal. They told him in their wheezing voices that they wouldn't let him heal because they, themselves, could never heal. The man was already bitter and angry with his people, the Ree-Kyae were excellent at taking negative feelings, and nurturing them, helping them grow into pure hatred. The man soon hated every Varian in Arathia, wanting nothing but to kill them, no, not kill them, make them suffer as he was suffering. Finally, the man agreed to do what the Ree-Kyae had wanted. They fastened a metal shackle around his ankle and lead him up to the hole that was directly under The Crystal Heart."

"He stuck his arm through the opening, there was heat radiating from The Crystal Heart, but it felt good on his skin after being locked in a cold, damp cave for so long, and he didn't burn like the Ree-Kyae did. He climbed out of the hole; the shackle clinked on the jagged rock wall as he emerged. Nothing was said by him, or the Ree-Kyae, as he approached The Crystal Heart; he slowly extended his arm. He walked closer to the heart, his eyes were tearing up from the sheer brightness of the light, his fingers were outstretched, he wanted to touch The Crystal Heart, wanted to feel it in his hand. He continued walking forward to the center of the light, and his pace quickened."

The fire showed a different man now, same features, but he was beaten, bruises outlined the wounds that he had sustained and he was covered in dried blood. He no longer stood tall and erect but was hunched over, his muscle definition had faded, and he was still naked as he walked over to a ball of light, the center being about the size of his fist.

"The traitor cupped his hands and extended them towards the center of the light. Despite the heat radiating from the heart, the crystal itself was cool to the touch. He used his fingers to caress the heart, felt every crack, every indentation, every vein and every bulge. What was even stranger to the man was that The Crystal Heart was still beating as if it were alive, with each beat of pulsating light, the heat grew and lessened, it was amazing. He couldn't believe he was touching the source of all the light in Arathia. He grabbed The Crystal Heart and tugged at it, trying to move it, but it was stuck in the air. He felt around to see if it was connected to anything, if there was something keeping it in place. Nothing could be felt by the man, but he didn't give up. He had his own plan, he hated the Varian People for what they had done to him, but he also hated the Ree-Kyae for keeping him captive, for not allowing his wounds to heal. He wanted to take The Crystal Heart down into the caves and tunnels of the Ree-Kyae, he wanted to destroy them, and then he wanted to destroy The Crystal Heart itself. He wanted both the Varians and the Ree-Kyae to suffer for what they had done to him."

The fire was showing a close up of his hands, surrounded in divine light and clutching at a human heart, pure white, radiating the light. The heart was somehow brighter than the light that was pouring out. The hands started pulling at the heart, yanking and tugging in every direction as his fingernails scraped across it, but the heart wouldn't budge. The image zoomed out enough to show the man's face, it was twisted with anger, his lips were pulled back revealing his teeth and a vain on his forehead throbbed as he tried to move the heart. His head turned as if he was looking around for something.

"The man was getting angry, he searched for something that could possibly move the heart. The traitor wasn't bright, and no one knew that the heart could be broken; everyone assumed that it was a constant in their world. He found a femur bone nearby; it was almost complete, one of the ends had been gnawed on and was splintered."

The fire showed the man picking up the bone, it was the size of an adults, and he clutched it in his hands holding the splintered end, which left the other side bulbous. His face adopted an even more twisted look, his teeth were bared, and his eyes squinted as he tried to focus on the heart in the center of the light.

"He swung the bone hard as he could at The Crystal Heart and it shattered." Bright white sparks shot out of the side and the fire went back to a very dark blue, the figure of the man was barely visible as one of the white sparks headed towards his face. "One of the shards ricocheted off of the mountain behind the heart and came back, it jetted to the man's face and had enough force to pierce his eye, and embed itself in his brain. That's the largest known shard of The Crystal Heart. Legend has it that the skull, the shard still inside of it, is kept by the leader of the Ree-Kyae so The Crystal Heart can never be reassembled."

The fire went out.

Chapter One

Fair Hero (Kinley)

Kinley was sitting on a petrified log by the river that his nomadic tribe was following, they were soon to leave, and he wasn't supposed to be wondering off by himself. Already at the age between child and adult, Kinley has shown promise to become a great fisher, but he was always lost in his thoughts. Kinleys world was dark, and not in a brooding angst way, that's how his entire planet was. It was dark since the start of time, then it was light for a little while thanks to The Crystal Heart, then somebody smashed The Crystal Heart and the shards of it haven't been recovered, no one has even tried looking for them, because reassembling it was impossible.

He did this often, sat aside the river his tribe was navigating by, Kinley felt connected to water. The

The Crystal Heart: Beginnings

Varian people were supposed to feel connected to fire; it's used so often among the Varian nomadic tribes and it stands for what every Varian child strives to be, bright, dangerous, useful and passionate about what they do. The storytellers use flame to illumistrate their stories, it is customary for newly joined couples to have a small fire in their tent the first time they make love to symbolize the passion and heat they want their relationship to have. Every meal is around a fire, if not for the damage fire can do it would be the only form of light the Varians used.

However, water, water, thought Kinley, *water is the only thing that can put out fire, water tells fire what it can and can't do. The storytellers cannot illumistrate when it's raining, after all.* Kinley gazed into the river, as far as he could see in the darkness that was his home, it seemed to go on forever. He stood up from the log and walked over to the bank. He wanted to touch the water, and feel it on his skin, he wasn't to go near it though, the depths and darkness have given birth to far too many violent creatures since The Crystal Heart was shattered. Fish as long as his arm, and twice as thick, with scales like bones and teeth the size of his thumb. Eels as thin as a blade with one spiral bone jutting out from their faces that would burrow into your skin and lay their eggs inside your body, the eels would die and their eggs would hatch and eat their host from the inside out, and those weren't even the most frightening of the creatures.

Kinley continued to stare down longingly at the water for longer than he should, wishing that The Crystal Heart hadn't been destroyed, that he could see more than a few arms lengths in front of him without assistance from flame or glow-grub. He wished his nomadic tribe would no longer wander, he wanted to be stationary, he wanted stability, and he wanted to no longer fear the Ree-Kyae. That is why they were nomadic anyway. To run from the Ree-Kyae, if they couldn't find the Varians then they couldn't steal them and take them as slaves. The Ree-Kyae wouldn't be able to use them as entertainment, pitting Varian neighbors against each other until the death, only for their amusement.

There was no point in worrying about that though; the constant relocation of their lifestyle was working for the moment. Kinley turned with a sigh; it was never an easy thing to tear his eyes from the water. He trekked the trail through the sparse crumbling weeds and dead dry moss, keeping his eyes on the ground directly below him. His mother would be worried about him, definitely upset. She was going to try to push him again.

"You should find a nice girl, settle down, and most importantly, move into your own tent." He heard that repeatedly before he slept. He would have left already except his mother was unwed, she had nobody to look after her and she needed him around.

His mother was beautiful enough; she could get a husband very easily if she wanted one. She had gorgeous flowing black hair; it was down to the small of her back. Her eyes were a bright and vibrant blue, the color of water. This was a feature he hadn't inherited, the base color of his eyes were a rusty brown, the same as just about every other Varian in Arathia. The only difference were the flecks of color in his eyes, they were cyan flecks around the pupil in the iris.

Well it makes for an interesting contrast, he thought

as he walked. The next reason he didn't meet a girl and move out was that none he saw interested him. Most of the Varian girls in Arathia looked the same, their eyes were the same color, and their hair was cropped to their shoulders, all dark hair, all with porcelain skin that shone bright. Not like his mother at all, his mother seemed to be from an entirely different land. However, she was born in Arathia to Arathian Varians.

He found a rock to kick on his way home; it was lying on the path in front of him. It was an odd shape, lopsided, round on one end, but sharp, and pointed on the other. It wasn't a large rock, about the size of his little finger. He stopped on the path, picked the rock up and inspected it. The rock looked like it was made of two different materials, one side was a dark gray splattered with bits of black, the other end, the pointed end, was metallic silver.

He ran his finger on the point, wanting to see how sharp it was. He felt a stinging in his finger, hot liquid poured from a deep gash. "That's sharp!" he said to no one as he stuck his finger in his mouth. He expected the rock to be jagged, but not something that would slice directly through his skin.

He pulled a small piece of leather out from his back pocket and wrapped the strange rock in it, then returned it to his pocket, hoping it wouldn't slice through the thick material.

That would definitely be a good weapon, he thought as he continued to walk down the path. Finally, the camp was in sight and his finger had stopped bleeding, though it was still stinging. He walked past a couple of families packing and loading their tents and supplies.

"Kinley, where have you been, we're just about to leave," A young woman about Kinley's age trotted to his side and walked next to him as he made his way to his tent, "your mother has been looking for you everywhere, you know she can't get everything together by herself."

Kinley rolled his eyes, he didn't have to be told how much his mother depended on him, but what would he tell Arissa? "Listen, you know how I get. Arissa, I found something."

"Oh, what is it? Something pretty for your future wife?" Arissa asked, batting her eyelashes at him.

"Ugh, there is no way that *you* are my future wife," Kinley said, "you're my sister in every way but blood, that's just gross."

Arissa laughed, "Yeah, thinking of you in any romantic way is just… gross." Her mouth said one thing but Kinley noticed something in her eyes, something that made him think she was lying.

She is pretty, he thought looking her up and down, *but every Arathian girl is pretty, they all look the same and Arissa is no exception.*

That was the truth, Arissa had the same shoulder length hair, the same eyes, the same moonshine skin, she was pretty, but she was average.

"I'll show you once we are alone," he winked at her, "it's something I don't want anyone else to know about."

"Awe, you make me feel special." Arissa stuck her tongue out at Kinley and he smiled back.

They talked for a while longer as they finished the short walk to the place where Kinleys family tent was still standing. His mother was outside batting at a support pole with a stick she most likely found lying on the ground. The pole stood firm and she was already breaking out in a sweat. She dug one end of the stick into the ground, using the other to steady herself; she wiped the sweat from her golden forehead and looked up. A smile broke across her face as she saw Kinley and Arissa making their way to the tent through the darkness.

"Hey honey," She said, "how was your walk?"

"It was fine Ma; you didn't start packing up without me did you?"

She looked around their temporary home; the sweat was already re-beading on her forehead. Everything looked the same, as when Kinley left. "No, I was just... cleaning up." She smiled at him. She had been trying to pack up before he returned, and she knew that he knew it, but was teasing her.

"Oh," he said, "well you did a very good job cleaning up. Why don't you go visit with Keeva, Arissa and I can pack everything up."

"Awe, thank you sweetie, that's a great idea." She said dropping the stick that was in her hand. She smiled at Arissa "Take care of my baby boy." She threw a wink her way.

Arissa blushed and looked down at her feet. Her eyes were barely visible under her bangs; they darted between Kinley and his mother. "No worries," she said to Kinley's mother, "he never gets into any trouble when he is with me."

Enat, Kinleys mother, turned and walked towards Keeva's tent. "Come inside!" Kinley said holding the tent flap open with his left hand and motioning for Arissa to enter with his right.

"Now, if you touch it you have to be very careful. I sliced my finger open on it earlier." He pulled the bundle of leather out of his back pocket and unfolded it gently; the rock lay directly in the center. Arissa's eyes locked onto it and studied it; Kinley could see it's reflection in her eyes.

He picked up the rock and noticed that it felt different from any other rock he has ever held… it felt alive.

There was almost a pulsation radiating from it, reverberating through his skin. Remembering the sharp tip and the gouge in his finger, Kinley looked down and, to his amazement, the wound had already healed; there wasn't even a thin red line; no sign there was a mark at all.

Arissa looked at him, puzzlement showing on her face, "I thought you said this thing cut you?"

"It did." Kinley stated, still trying to figure out what had happened. He tested the spot on his finger where, earlier, the blood had flowed. He set the curious stone down still staring at his finger. He poked it, squeezed his fingertip, rubbed it and he couldn't feel any difference, there were no severed, or dead, nerve endings.

"That's why I brought it back, I figured it would make a good weapon, it cut through my skin so easily, but maybe I imagined it." Kinley picked the rock back up; he passed the tip over his finger in the same place, not applying any pressure. A very thin red line appeared as it passed over, for the second time he had used the rock to slice his skin open. Arissa looked horrified.

"What are you doing, are you insane?" she asked him, a slight hint of panic in her voice.

"Just watch it," he replied, "I want to see what happens, and no, I'm not insane."

They sat and watched Kinley's fingertip. The

red line was still there but this time Kinley felt no pain. The blood started to drip off his finger, he followed a droplet as it passed around his finger and clung to it, at the nail bed, not wanting to let go. Then it fell like a crimson jewel and splashed onto the dirt below, it was absorbed into the earth almost instantly. The pulsating of the stone in his hand intensified as if the blood had awoken it from hibernation.

Arissa and Kinley sat there, staring at his finger, but no more drops fell. The blood had begun to dry; Kinley could feel it pulling at his skin. He stuck the finger into his mouth, sucking on it. He pulled his finger out of his mouth with a pop, and Arissa let out a gasp.

Again, there was nothing there, no thin red line, no white scar, no trace of the cut on his finger. They looked down where Kinley's blood had touched the earth expecting to see a wet spot but there was not even a stain, no trace of red whatsoever.

"It's like the earth is thirsty and your blood quenched its thirst. Even on battle fields there are blood stains afterwards." Arissa said monotone.

"I can't see how this is possible. Obviously this thing is no good for a weapon. Anything it strikes will look unaffected a short time later. What did I pick up?" The last part was him thinking aloud but Arissa assumed that he was talking to her. "I have no idea, but I think you should put it back where you found it. I can't imagine any good coming from that thing."

"Yeah, you're right." Kinley said, only to appease her, there was no way he was putting the rock back out in the open, this was his now, he found it.

"Let's get started taking this place apart, put that rock back in your pocket for now, I guess just dropping it on our way out of here will be good enough." Arissa said as she stood up and brushed the dirt from her knees. She headed over to the poles and started breaking down Kinley's family tent. Kinley noticed a small rock sitting on the ground by his feet, he reached down slyly and picked it up to drop later on.

*   *   *

The group was mostly walking; the most important were being pulled by their servants in wheeled carts. They were following their river until they reached the Trading Post, where the five rivers met. Each river symbolized a valued character trait for the Varian people. The one they were following now meant "Strength"; it was one of the most difficult rivers to follow. The terrain that surrounds this river is hard to travel, there are steep sloping hills and jagged mountains, deep gullies and roads that could be better described as loose gravel scattered on top of dry sand. Kinley noticed that Arissa kept an eye on him.

She is probably watching me to see if I am going to drop the rock. Kinley thought to himself as he walked beside his mother. He took the rock from his pocket that he picked up from the floor of his tent, and dropped it, it's a good thing that Arissa wasn't directly behind him or she would have been able to tell it was a farce. The rock he dropped was plain; it was a dull brown, smaller than the other as well, about half the size of the original. This rock was almost completely round, not elongated, or brought to a point at the end.

Kinley stole a glance at Arissa, she winked at him and smiled, the relief showed in her eyes. *I am so sorry Arissa,* he thought, *you know you are the last person I would ever want to lie to.* Almost considered an adult, he grabbed his mother's hand and helped her along the path. He wondered what she would say if she knew what he had in his back pocket, wondered how she would react knowing he had already cut himself twice with this tool.

There is no day and night in a world where the sun never rises, people are awake until they are tired, then they sleep and wake when they are rested. The nomadic tribe stopped to rest for a while and to sleep. They built a fire and the council elders gathered around with the tribes' storyteller, Caedmon; he started reciting the tale of the Man-God. The Man-God gave Kinleys people the light, and the Ree-Kyae took it away. Everyone knew the story, and rarely, Caedmon would tell it to the people that belonged to the nomadic tribe. Illumistrations were reserved for the council; sometimes Kinley would sneak back to the circle and watch from behind a cart, though if he was caught, he could have been banished. Not this time, however, he was too busy setting up camp, his mother was cooking their meal over a small fire right outside the tent.

Kinley had gone to the river with a few others and caught a few of the monstrous beasts for the tribe. These fish were very long, twice the size of his arm and almost as thick as his head. The one he kept was a deep red color with a blue bioluminescent stripe running down each side of its body, and it had a very vicious looking set of teeth. The ones at the center of its beak shaped mouth started longer than his longest finger and were needle thin, as you got closer to the corners of its mouth they got shorter, thicker, and serrated. It had paper-thin spiny fins running along the top and bottom of its body and the tailfin of the fish curved in on itself with wicked looking spikes. Its pectoral fins looked almost vestigial; they were long but not very wide, the creature swam in an eel-like back and forth motion.

Enat had invited Keeva over to their fire to share their meal, the two women were chattering to themselves. *Most likely talking the tribe's gossip,* thought Kinley not remotely interested in who was sleeping with whom, or who was having problems in their relationship. Kinley had invited Arissa over as well, she was always happy to eat with him and his mother. The fish meat was very bland, except for the faint sour aftertaste that was left on the palate, but it filled an empty stomach, and that's the important part.

"So you dropped the rock, huh?" Arissa said to Kinley shortly after arriving. Kinley looked down; he wasn't exactly the best liar so he didn't want to make eye contact.

"Yes, I dropped the rock." He wasn't completely lying to her. He did drop *a* rock, just not the one that she meant. *That's a bad excuse,* Kinley thought, *lying is still lying and I know which rock she means.* He was already feeling the guilt of betraying the trust of his friend, but he couldn't just drop the rock, he had to find out more about it.

"Good," Arissa said, "that thing was creepy, there wasn't even a scar, it's like it never even cut you."

I know, Kinley was trying to reason with himself for not dropping the rock, *but maybe if it dealt a fatal blow, like slicing through somebody's throat or jabbing straight into his or her heart, it wouldn't heal.* "Yeah, good thing I dumped it off." is what he actually said.

He stuck his finger in his back pocket, and fingered the leather in which his strange tool was wrapped. Kinley felt, at any moment, Arissa would force his hand out, reach in and take the leather, guilt washed over him. There was a strange heat radiating from his pocket, not enough to burn him, but enough for him to notice the difference.

He brought his finger out of his pocket and could still feel the leather on his skin. The warmth lingered for a moment. Kinley reached down to his fish, feeling almost full, he tried to take his mind off the guilt that he felt for lying to Arissa. Kinley brought the fish to his mouth and took a bite of the meat.

"...isn't that right Kinley?" his mother said looking at him. "Huh. What? Sorry Ma, I wasn't paying attention." Kinley pulled one of the little bones from between his teeth. "Oh, I was just telling Keeva about this fish, how long it was when you pulled it out, not one I have ever seen before."

"Yeah a new one, I have never pulled one like that out of the river before, I am not sure anyone has. Damn thing, it almost bit my hand clean off." He remembered he had been lost in his own head and that Arissa was sitting in front of him. A blank stare inhabited her face, Kinley didn't know what to make if it. Had he said something while he was spacing out, had he been talking about the rock?

"It... it... almost bit your hand off?" she stammered.

"Well, it's no big deal." Kinley said, poking her with his hand, it smelled like the fish, Arissa noticed and wrinkled her nose.

"Kinley, you've got to be more careful... and wash your hands they stink."

"I just pulled this monster beast out of the river and you want me to go stick my hands in again?" Kinley shouted pulling another mouthful of fish to his face, "Give this guy's brother a chance to avenge his death? I think not, he'll have both my hands, then who will catch you fish to eat?" He took a bite.

He looked around the camp, Kinley noticed every detail that the lack of natural lighting would allow; aside from the rocky pieces of the banks of this river, this site looked the same. It had skeletons of plants only shin high and dirt everywhere, it looked like a desert, aside from the river that wound through it just a little ways away from Kinley.

It looks so empty here; he thought to himself, *I wonder what it was like when The Crystal Heart was up.* "Ma," he said interrupting Keeva as she elaborated on the latest scandals, "can you tell me again? I am sure Arissa would like to hear too."

Enat looked over to him, "Hold on honey, Keeva and I were talking." Keeva finished her story as Arissa and Kinley sat patiently. "What's your favorite part of the story?" she asked him. She had been there many times with Kinley when his mother recounted the past. She told them about the skies, they were actually a light and beautiful blue. She told them that the clouds were white and that there used to be green moss covering the ground instead of rocks and dirt. She told them about the animals that used to live there; when The Crystal Heart was shattered, the Ree-Kyae killed them, and what the Ree-Kyae hadn't killed had starved to death.

Kinleys favorite parts of the stories were the parts involving the waters. They were a bright blue mixed with green, only a little darker then the skies.

His mother looked over to them, "Kinley, what did you want to hear about?"

Keeva looked over at her, Enat wasn't a storyteller, so her stories weren't accompanied by illumistrations, but they were still entertaining. Kinley spoke up, he still hadn't answered Arissa's question aloud.

"Tell me about the oceans and rivers, they are my favorite part." Kinley winked at Arissa as Enat began her story.

"The waters of the light, huh, I can do that. First off, when you looked out onto the waters of light they shimmered as if millions of diamonds floated at the surface. The waters were a beautiful blue green and crystal clear. You could see under the water. Every detail was exposed; every rock, every fish, and every plant was visible to the naked eye. There were different fish then, and they came in an uncountable number of different shapes and colors. There were fish that were as flat as the blade of the sword, they were yellow in the center and the yellow was outlined in ice blue, which faded out to a bright and vibrant red. There were fish as short as your little finger and as long as your leg, none of them like the ones we have today, they all lacked the sharp teeth and fins; they had no need for the living light. Sometimes when The Crystal Heart was putting off a lot of heat we would go in the water and swim with the fish, there was no danger. I can remember standing in the cool waters; the fish would come to me and nibble on my toes as I stood on the rocks. Do you remember that Keeva?"

Keeva looked at Enat; her eyes were lost as her thoughts wandered. She was only half listening to Enat's story, and mostly remembering the experiences herself. She and Enat had been best friends since before they were Kinley and Arissa's age, they had done and felt what Enat was describing on many occasions together. Keeva missed the freedom, missed the warmth of The Crystal Heart on her skin and the cool water contrasting it. She missed the sweet little fish that used to nibble on their fingers and toes; she missed them because she knew them.

"Yes, I remember." was all she said and Enat continued with her story.

"The waters of light were beautiful, right along the edge was always a layer of fine white sand, nothing grew there but it was so beautiful, and the fine sand felt silky when it touched you. Keeva and I used to lie on the sand after a swim, it would stick to our skin and we would just feel the beating heat from The Crystal Heart on our faces. After a while we would get up and walk back to our village, when we left the sand we felt the spongy moss under our feet, it was warm and moist and springy."

"We ran, and we could feel the muscles in our legs coil. We ran fast, trying to get to the village before the other, making it into a game, it was all carefree. We could feel the wind rushing past our faces and with that; we felt the freedom in our souls. The sparkling waters were in the background; we passed the trees as we ran. The colors of their leaves, the bright purples and blues, yellows greens and oranges, they all blurred together. We saw shapes in them, there were angry faces, happy faces, animals and men."

"It was all so beautiful!"

*   *   *

"Come this way." A voice said to him he was walking a clear pathway edged by trees, the one he always visited in his dreams. The foliage was lush and multicolored, like rainbows that sprang from the ground; the trees seemed too reach past the skies. He ran through a patch of moss, subconsciously remembering the stories his mother had told him and Arissa before he had gone to sleep. Kinley was at the bank of a river, the same river he was traveling on with his tribe. Only now it appeared different, it was blue and green. Kinley could see under the water, he could see the fish, the plants, the rocks, he could see every little detail. Still, for some reason, he felt as if he had to run.

"Kinley, our lives," the voice said, "they are one and the same, maybe not yet, but they become the same." Kinley continued down the river, the moss now squashing under his feet.

"I don't know who you are, why are you chasing me?" Kinley yelled to the disembodied voice behind him.

"Kinley," it said, "I am not chasing you. I am you."

Kinley woke up; his brow was wet with sweat. He rubbed it on the dried moss pillow that was under his head. He was upset with himself.

What in the hell was that? He thought, *and why am I dreaming it?*

He felt the shard, still in his back pocket; it was pulsating, a tiny bit if heat radiating from it. He ignored it and went back to sleep.

*　　*　　*

Kinley woke up to find that his family tent was already half packed away. This was new to him, different. He hoped his mother hadn't started packing up without him. There is no way she could have had it this far broken down already. Kinley looked around, he was lying on his crude mattress, stuffed with dried moss and any other form of former greenery that was found, he looked up but there was no movement.

What's going on? He wondered to himself. His mother was still sound asleep on her dried foliage mattress just a little bit away from him. He heard rustling around the sides of the tent. He reached in his back pocket for the pulsating shard. It was still there, safely wrapped in leather. His face suddenly flushed with embarrassment.

Why would someone be after this, it's nothing important? He thought. He crept up from his bed, over to where the tent was rattling. He pulled back the side.

His face was met with a startled expression. "Arissa?" he asked questioningly, "What are you doing?"

"Everyone is breaking down already, I saw that yours hadn't moved at all and came over to help you, but you and your mother were still sleeping, I didn't want to wake you up. Not until I needed to anyway." She said.

Kinley's face was the one to show surprise now; he couldn't have slept for more than half of what he normally does when they stop to rest. "Everyone's packing up already? Why? What's wrong?"

"Nothing's wrong, it's the same as every other time that we wake up. Kinley, what's wrong with you?"

"I couldn't have been sleeping that long, It feels like I just went to sleep." Kinley yawned near the end of his sentence, Arissa almost found it difficult to hear what he was saying.

"Well you were tossing and turning when I came over." Arissa said as she raised an eyebrow, "What were you dreaming about anyway?"

"Nothing important," Kinley said, "you can go back to your tent now, I can take it down the rest of the way, and I have to get Ma up now anyway."

Arissa stuck out her tongue, "You're welcome." She said as she turned around and walked to her own family's tent.

Kinley stretched in the darkness, and then sat down for a moment, he was willing himself the energy to get up and start the task of breaking everything down. His mother stepped out of the tent humming; she was obviously well rested. "Hey Ma, how are you doing, sleep well?" he asked as he rolled his mattress around his pillow and tied the misshapen bundle. "I slept very well. I dreamt of when The Crystal Heart was whole, only I wasn't as young. Everything was beautiful again. Sweetie, do you want some help breaking everything down?" she asked him.

"I already had some," he said, "Arissa was here when I woke up and almost all the work was done already, all I have now is the tent and what's in it. You can go ahead and talk your gossip with the others if you want to." Kinley tossed his mother a wink.

He finished packing the loose stuff and retreated into the tent, so he could have a moment alone. He reached into his back pocket and pulled out the little leather bundle.

Again, he unwrapped it and examined the rock. He felt the strange pulsating and looked deeply into the shiny part of it; tried to find a line around it, to show that it was two different pieces, and not one whole. He could find no evidence but the pulsating seemed to be stronger from the metallic end. He couldn't feel it as strongly on the side with the gray and black rock.

Kinley closed his eyes and put it close to his ear, trying to see if the rock made a sound, there was nothing. He was becoming obsessed with the rock, with the pulsating and with the strange heat that radiated from it. Kinley looked around on the dirt floor of the tent, he found what he was looking for, a second rock, and this new one was relatively flat. He grabbed his rock by the rounded gray and black end and raised it over his head. Kinley brought the pointed end down, as hard as he could, on the flat rock. It split in half and his rock plunged into the dirt, not even swayed by the friction.

Kinley wrapped his rock back up in the leather, relieved that he hadn't broken it. He didn't know why, but he felt that there was something special about this pointed, jagged rock. Kinley looked down at the hole his rock had created in the ground, but something seemed off about it.

He felt the surface around the hole with his little finger, put it inside the hole and was surprised to feel a smooth surface. Kinley scooped around and under the puncture, dirt spilled from the gaps between his fingers. Kinley looked down in his hand; he picked up the whole thing, completely undisturbed. He set it down on the ground and pulled the entire perforation out of the dirt. A few pieces of soil still clung to it, other than that it was completely clear. He pulled a water skin from the belt around his waist and started washing it off.

He soon held an object that looked like an icicle, it was perfectly clear and in the same shape, he could have picked it off one of the dead trees during the cold season, only it was not cold at all. It was smoother than anything he had ever felt, and the part where the pointed end of the rock was, came to a blunt end. Kinley ran his finger over the end.

Not sharp at all, I wonder, he thought to himself, *if the inside is still the same shape as the rock.*

He slipped the rock into this new material, it fit perfectly into it. He scraped the pointed end against the leather, not wanting to try this out with his finger this time. It was unaffected; apparently, the point of the rock didn't extend outside the hard clear material.

He wanted to run from his tent to Arissa's, to apologize to her for deceiving her by dropping the other rock. He wanted to tell her about his dream, that he thought it and the rock were connected. He wanted to show her how he made this new material and wanted to see if he could make more, but he didn't. Instead, he stood up and wrapped the clear material, still on the pointed edge of the rock, and the rock itself back up in the leather, and re-placed it in his back pocket.

Kinley broke down the tent, and loaded everything up into his family's wagon. Surprisingly, he wasn't the last one at the meeting spot. This was the point where they would get the motivational speech to keep moving. The leader of the tribe, Fallyn, stood in the center of the circle, the elders of the tribe were gathered around him in another circle, and they faced out towards the people staring at them.

"Here we go again," Fallyn started as he looked around at the tribe that was gathering around the group of men, "the Ree-Kyae are very close to us, you can catch the scent of them on the wind. We need to start spending less time in each place, at least until we are far enough from them."

Fallyn stopped for a moment and let what he said sink in. Usually his speeches followed the course of I know everyone is tired, but we have to keep moving. This was something different, and the people of the tribe didn't like that. It meant something was up, it was new, and it was different.

Kinley stood there for a moment, looking around for his mother, she was chattering off to the side with Keeva. Enat had a look in her eyes that Kinley hadn't seen in a long time, it was a spark, for a moment she wasn't a beaten woman anymore. Her eyes searched around the tribe and when they met Kinley's, then the same look she had worn before returned to her face. No Spark, eagerness, or excitement could be seen anymore, just a woman, tan, blue eyes, long hair, and beaten.

Now that's strange. Kinley thought. He chalked it up to the excitement of Fallyn's news and the possibility of a fight. Fallyn began to speak again, "If the Ree-Kyae catch up with us, we have to defend ourselves. I want all the men to walk at the back of the group, take comfort in knowing that your children and your partners are safely ahead, and you are standing between them and the Ree-Kyae." With that, the group in the center dispersed and the nomadic tribe began to move on to the Varian Trading Post where the five rivers meet.

Chapter Two

Half Way There

Kinley traveled at the back of the group with the rest of the men. He hated leaving his mother behind, but he took comfort in Fallyn's words, knowing that he stood between the Ree-Kyae and his mother. Arissa tried to linger near the back of the group as well, to talk to him as they walked but she was shoved off and told that she was a liability. That never kept her away for too long though, she would fall past the children, to the back of the women and eventually start drifting back towards Kinley. In one of their short lived conversations she had brought up the rock, the one that she thought Kinley had dropped. The question she asked had kept Kinley thinking the rest of the walk.

"What do you think it was?"

"I don't know," Kinley replied, "but it wasn't normal."

"What do you mean it wasn't normal? I mean, yeah, it was shiny and sharp, but still, it was just a rock." Arissa said.

"Yeah, a rock, one that cuts you, but you don't stay cut."

"Maybe we were just seeing things," Arissa suggested, "and maybe it didn't cut you at all, I bet you that rock was really dirty, maybe it just had some red sand on it. You did find it by the river, right?"

Kinley grunted a yes, and drifted off into his own thoughts while Arissa walked beside him, "You know, once when I was little, I was walking down by the river and I slipped on a wet rock. My knees stung so bad, I could have sworn that they had been stripped of the skin; I looked down and saw red all over my legs. I started to cry, because I thought something was seriously wrong with me. My mom picked me up and tried to stop me from crying, but I wouldn't even look down at my legs. Finally, after what seemed like forever at the time, my mom coaxed me into looking down. Just as I did, she took a wet cloth and wiped red sand off my legs. I thought she was magic." Arissa giggled, "It only took me a little while to realize that when I slipped, my legs just landed in the red sand and there was no blood at all." Kinley nodded.

"I bet you," Arissa kept going, "that there was some of that red sand on the rock, and that when you drug the rock over your finger you just got a line of red sand on it. I bet that you didn't cut it at all and it just stung because the rock was sharp and you had pressure on your skin."

Kinley didn't bring up any of the points he

wanted to, like the rock had cut him twice, or that he tasted the blood in his mouth, and the biggest one he wanted to bring up was that the rock had created its own sheath, just from being plunged into the dirt. "Yeah, you're probably right, but," he said, "just out of curiosity, what do you think could do that, if it really did cut me, I mean?"

Arissa thought for a moment "I don't really know weapons well, why don't you ask that guy over there." She nodded to a big muscular person who was glaring at her, probably about to come over and shoo her away again. "He kind of reminds me of the animals your mom tells us about, when The Crystal Heart was still up, big and vicious; I can see why he is near the back of the men. What did your mom say that animal was called, the brown one, with all the fur…?" Arissa trailed off, hoping that Kinley would remember. Lost in his own thoughts, he wasn't paying much attention to what Arissa had to say. He barely noticed that the man from the back, the one who they had just been talking about, was coming closer to the front.

Arissa noticed though, she shot the muscular man a glare as she retreated into the crowd of women. The man didn't stop, he kept walking over to Kinley, questions still running through his own mind, Kinley didn't even notice. "Hey!" the man said. His voice grew in annoyance when Kinley didn't show any acknowledgment.

"Hey you." Kinley's head snapped up from his feet.

"Yes?"

"You need to keep your girlfriend with the women; she can't be back here with you. If the Ree-Kyae decided to show up while she was back here she could get hurt."

"I am not having her come back here, she is doing that all on her own, and she isn't my girlfriend." Kinley answered.

The man's voice showed even more annoyance, Kinley was thinking that the person didn't like to be corrected.

"The point is that she can't be back here, just send her away when she tries to..."

The man said more but Kinley ignored him, he wasn't interested in what the man had to say, he was too busy thinking about the rock that was sheathed in glass as hard as diamonds, and wrapped in leather sitting snug in his back pocket. Kinley and his group walked for a lot longer than they normally did, trying to gain some ground on the Ree-Kyae. When they finally stopped for a rest, the men were able to visit their loved ones in shifts.

Kinley was walking around trying to find his mother's tent. Eventually he found it, still bundled up, and parked behind Keeva's tent. He walked a little closer and could hear talking coming from behind the thick fabric that had been dyed a deep wine color.

"...can you imagine" Keeva's voice said.

"If the dreams are right, the heart is going to be pieced..." Enat said.

Kinley took a step forward in an attempt to hear well. "...but who is going to..." Keeva asked.

"I have no... but whoever... they aren't telling."

Kinley started getting frustrated, normally he wouldn't sneak up and eavesdrop on Enat, but the look in her eyes before they left made him think that she wouldn't tell him what was going on. She was definitely hiding something when she noticed his gaze and completely changed the look on her face.

Still not being able to hear very much Kinley stepped forward, because he was not looking down he didn't know what he was walking on. A grinding noise sounded from under his feet as two rocks scraped together loudly. He heard his mother in the tent, hushing Keeva.

Great, he thought, *now I am not going to be able to hear anything.*

Keeva pulled the flap to her tent back a little, to see who was stepping around it. A look of relief crossed her face when she saw that it was only Kinley. Enat peered over Keeva's shoulder and a smile spread across her face.

"Hi baby, on your break from guard duty?" she said, "Any sign of the Ree-Kyae?"

"No Ma, no sight, you sure can smell them, only when the wind hits the wrong way though. They really do smell like death, it's disgusting, one of the guys threw up." Kinley chuckled clearly amused by this.

Enat stepped out of the tent and walked over to him, there was a big embrace with more strength then Kinley had ever felt her put into a hug. Something was definitely different about his mother, and whatever it was, had been so since they left. Kinley felt a hand on his shoulder; he turned his head slightly and saw Arissa's moonlight skinned fingers resting there.

Kinley wanted to talk to his mother more, to try to find the underlying cause of what was going on in her head, but Arissa had ruined that moment.

"Hey, Arissa, how are you doing?" His mother

let go of the embrace and he halfheartedly turned to greet her.

"I need to talk to you." She said grabbing onto his arm and pulling him away from Enat and Keeva. "That boulder man came over to my tent. He told me to stay away from you and that you didn't even want me back there. What a jerk!"

"Arissa, you aren't supposed to be there. If we were attacked and you were there, the others would think of you as a risk. They don't want you in the way, I know exactly what he was saying to you; he came over and started harassing me because you were there. Maybe you should just stay up front with the others."

Arissa was speechless.

"Look, all I am saying is that maybe you should just wait until I have my breaks when we stop."

"Kinley," she said, "I don't want anything to happen to you." She looked away from him, embarrassed. She sat down on the ground, legs crossed, and elbows resting on her knees. Her hair hung down over her face as her head tilted forward until she was looking at the ground.

Kinley made a noise as if he was sucking air in through his teeth. "Arissa, you don't have to worry about me. You are my best *friend*," he made sure to emphasize the word friend, "I am back there to protect my mother, Keeva, and you. How am I going to be able to protect you if you are right in the middle of the danger?"

Arissa's head snapped up, "You… protect… me? You are the one that needs the protection Kinley. Finding mutated rocks that are so sharp they cut your skin when they just barely touch you, pulling fish with teeth as long as your fingers out of the river with your bare hands, now I worry that you are going to either die or get captured by the Ree-Kyae, can you imagine anything worse than that?"

Kinley just stood there and stared at her. Her face was up, but her head was still cradled in her hands, her eyes were sparkling with tears. If she hadn't looked so hurt, pathetic, and worried he would be furious with her. He thought, and realized that yes, he had been attracting trouble lately, or from her perspective, it was trouble. She didn't know how important the rock was to him, he didn't think it was something evil, or mutated.

Catching the fish was something that he had to do, the people of the tribe had to eat and if he didn't catch the fish, then who would. It wasn't his fault the fish in all the rivers all had huge teeth and razor sharp fins. He wasn't going to find a fluffy and cuddly creature in this world, not since The Crystal Heart had been shattered. The Ree-Kyae hunting them down, that was just a normal thing; they were always on their tail, trying to pick off stragglers for their amusement. This was all stuff that just happened, just a part of life.

"Arissa, you are overreacting." He managed to get out; the tears in her eyes became more prominent. "What other fish are in the water, not the cute little ones from my mom's stories, and there isn't anything else to eat here. I have to catch the fish or we will starve, as for the Ree-Kyae, there is always that risk, they are always after us, at least we are meeting them head on this time as opposed to them sneaking up on us while we were sleeping. Seriously, it's no big deal, I will be fine, and I just need you to stay up with your group while I hang back with mine."

Arissa's head sunk back down dejectedly.

"Fine," she said in a stiff monotone voice, "if you aren't going to worry about yourself, then I sure as hell am not going to worry about you either." In one swift motion, Arissa stood up and stormed off to her tent.

Great, Kinley thought to himself, *now what am I going to do?* His posture changed, shoulders slumped down and his head was lowered when he walked into Keeva's camp. He looked as defeated as his mother normally did.

"Who died?" Enat asked as he walked in.

"Not right now, Ma." He said, "Let's just set up your tent and have something to eat."

"Not while you aren't here, Keeva has offered to put me up, and then I won't have to go around setting up and breaking down the tent. It's going to be so much easier." Enat laughed like there is nothing else she would rather do.

"We can eat though, that's for sure. How long is your break Kinley?" Keeva wondered.

Kinley shrugged, he really didn't know, he just assumed that when they needed him back at the back someone would be sent to get him.

"Can you go to the river and get us some fish? We ran out of the other one you caught." Enat said, her eyes met his but all he did was nod, he grabbed his empty bottle as he turned and walked towards the river. She knew this was what he needed, to be alone, to feel the water on his skin, even though it was ice cold water, it was still something that he enjoyed.

Enat watched him walk, when he got to the river's edge he made his way up the bank until he was completely covered in darkness.

Enat turned to Keeva "Now, weren't we talking about something important?"

*   *   *

Kinley walked along the water's edge for a little while, not wanting to think about anything other than where he was going, and there wasn't really much thought in that. He would have to soon; he knew that, because he couldn't just stay numb.

Catching fish required thought, if he didn't pull the lure hand out of the water fast enough, he could lose it. If he couldn't reach down and grab the fish fast enough, he would lose it. If he didn't bring the knife down on it fast enough, it would thrust, squirm, and snap its jaws trying to get at him, and who knows what he would lose then. Kinley found a boulder and took a seat on it, staring off over the river, willing his eyes to adjust better so he could see further, they didn't.

He strained his eyes and thought about what it would be like, with The Crystal Heart in place. He imagined the clouds in the sky, just as his mother had described, he tried to see the dark water before him, light blue and clear. He looked as deeply into it as his eyes would allow, imagining what the bottom would look like, pretending he could see little fish, yellow fading to blue fading to red, darting around rocks and plants. It wasn't working out to well for him.

I guess I better catch the fish and make my way back to camp, before someone comes looking for me and I don't even get a chance to eat.

Kinley stood up from his rock and walked over to the rivers bank. He started flipping over rocks, as many as he could find, searching for the bioluminescent glow-grubs that he would use to light the water as much as he could. He gathered a bunch of them, then reached to his waste, he untied the bottle from his belt and started stuffing as many of the little fat glowing creatures in as would fit. Once the bottle was full he tied some long woven fiber to it and, the other end, to his belt loop, then he tossed it into the water, he had a semi-well lit area.

He leaned over the riverbank and shoved his arm in as deep as it would go. Keeping his eyes just barely above the water, he paid close attention to the lit area, if he missed one tiny movement it could mean the end of his hand, or worse, his arm, and if the fish was strong enough, the end of his life.

He started wiggling his fingers under the water, trying to attract one of the river-beasts. A short time later, he got his chance.

He saw it approach from the side; this fish was long and very fat. It had four whiskers jutting out from the front of its face and every part of its skin put off an acidic green glow. For a moment, Kinley considered pulling his hand out of the water and not luring this fish any closer, with a color like that, its bound to be dangerous. Over time his worry faded and it was just another fish.

It swam closer to him, and Kinley hoisted his hand a little higher towards the top of the water, his fingers wiggled almost violently. The fish circled his hand twice; with his fingers still wiggling he started waving his hand back and forth to entice the fish to come at it.

The fish seemed to lose interest, the whiskers on its face twitched and it went the other way, moving out of the light. Kinley laid there, stunned, he had been working on improving his technique and when he waved his hand with his fingers, all of them wiggling, the fish normally went for it.

Kinley pulled his bioluminescent to another spot. He bent down and lowered his hand like before; nothing came close. He wiggled his fingers in the same pattern, hoping to attract something. Still nothing came; Kinley sighed and rolled his eyes. He felt a sting in his hand and looked down in time to see something green racing away from him.

All at once, his head felt fuzzy, Kinley sat up, soon whatever light the bioluminescence gave off faded to black. He started panicking and flailed his limbs until they wouldn't move anymore. Kinley fell to the side, his head hit something hard and he saw an explosion of red.

His field of vision was still black but he heard a voice, the same one from his dream, it was rhythmic and smooth as honey. Rich and full, the man's voice said "Kinley, wake up, open your eyes." Kinley lay there a while longer; he listened to the voice coaxing him awake.

"Who are you?" he mumbled, eyes still closed.

"Kinley I am you, and you are me, our hearts our one." The man's voice replied in its smooth tone.

Kinley's eyes opened, it was unbelievably bright by the river, he blinked repeatedly as his eyes adjusted, but he still couldn't see a thing.

"It's okay Kinley," the voice said, "just give it time, you'll make it out, just keep blinking."

Kinley did what the voice said and blinked his eyes a few more times, eventually he was able to see, and what an amazing sight he saw, everything was lit up, and he could see amazingly far, further than ever before.

The Rivers were clear, but he wasn't by them,

he was up on a mountain, and white light was radiating from behind him. He was warm as he looked out over the plains that he and his family walked. He could see the point where the five rivers met, the Varian Trading Post. Tents were set up everywhere and it was busy, the hustle and bustle surprised Kinley, he had never seen anything like it before.

He could see animals too, everywhere; there were herds of animals, of different shapes, sizes and colors. All of them were new things he had never seen with his own eyes, but had been described to him on many different occasions by his mother and Keeva, including a small group of the big, boulder-looking vicious ones that Arissa had compared the man who had approached and warned to keep her away. The man didn't look like this animal at all. Its fur was ragged and a deep chocolate brown, its eyes were huge and took up almost half its face. It walked on four legs and had a very long curved tail that ended with a pointed bone, obviously a weapon.

The group was surrounding a smaller animal, light blue in color, it was away from its group and seemed afraid, and it stood on only two legs but was nowhere near humanoid in form. Instead of arms it had four tentacles that all originated from the same spot. The tentacles wiggled in frustration as the animal stepped back and forth on its wide hoofed feet. Kinley turned away from the sight; he didn't want to see the smaller creature get killed and eaten.

"Don't turn away Kinley," The voice told him, "you are going to see a lot of death, some of it caused by your own hand, you must watch."

Kinley turned his head slightly just as the big brown creatures closed in on the little pale blue one.

The pointed bone at the end of its tail jabbed forward fast and hit the blue animal just above where its legs met; Kinley assumed this was the belly.

The other animals spring on the blue creature. Tails were lashing uncontrollably and the blue creature was no longer blue; it was covered in dark red blood. It screamed an ear-piercing scream as it fell to the ground. The boulder-like creatures lowered their heads and began feasting before it was dead. When the brown animals had their fill, they left the rest of the creature there.

Kinley started to turn his head back. "No," the voice said, "You need to learn the way that life works. There is always going to be something else coming along, it's how the planet recycles everything. Things live, they die, and then they help something else survive. Senseless murder is the reason that the Ree-Kyae don't belong here, and you need to understand that."

Kinley said nothing; he only turned his head back in the direction of the creature's corpse.

As he watched, he saw many different types of scavengers come to the corpse, eat their fill and then leave, eventually there was nothing left, even the bones had been gnawed on and eaten. Again, Kinley tried to turn away thinking that the circle had been completed but the voice chimed in.

"Life isn't finished blooming from this one death yet, you saw how it affected the animals but there are more living things on this planet."

Kinley rotated his head once again, and watched the spot where the creature had once been. He watched for what seemed a very long time, so long that eventually his legs got tired and he sat.

"There," the disembodied voice said, "can you see it?"

Kinley looked harder, and as he watched, a huge tree began to grow. One tiny twig grew, as the twig grew, branches swelled from it. Leaves of almost every color seemed to be exploding from the branches. Different hues of oranges, blues, yellows, purples, reds and greens took over the tree. Kinley continued to watch as the tree grew, eventually the Varian's came and sat under the tree, and so did many other animals. Smaller creatures built homes in the tree and raised their offspring there.

As long as Kinley had been sitting there, he wasn't tired or any older.

"Okay," said the voice, "did you learn what I meant?"

Kinley spoke, for what seemed like a first time in a long time, "Yes, everything has a purpose, the animal was killed to feed many others, it also fertilized the ground so that the tree could grow, once the tree grew it provided shade for people and animals along with many different homes for many different smaller creatures. Its death was necessary for other life to continue, and for new life to start."

"Now, do you see the reason that the Ree-Kyae don't belong here?" The voice asked.

"Is it because the Ree-Kyae give nothing back, they only take?" Kinley answered.

"Yes and no, that's part of the reason, but Kinley, there is much more to it than that. The Ree-Kyae kill senselessly. They do it for their entertainment, they do it because they are angry, and they don't do it to survive. Now I want you to turn around Kinley."

He followed the orders given to him and turned on his heels; he should have closed his eyes. There was an extremely bright light pulsating from behind him.

"This is The Crystal Heart, its whole and as you know, without it, this planet cannot grow."

Kinley stared at it as the voice continued to speak. "As you know, The Crystal Heart has been shattered, but it can be repaired, the problem is it has to be placed back together by a descendant of the person who destroyed it. Every piece must be found and grouped together. Step closer."

Kinley listened again, in awe of what he was looking at. His eyes burned as he continued to stare at the heart, but he couldn't look away, he couldn't blink, he took a step closer to it, trying to grasp what was going on.

"Come on Kinley; move closer, this is very important." The voice said. Kinley walked closer, he was almost within touching distance of the heart. He felt it pulsate and felt the heat radiate. Though not hot enough to burn him, a pleasant warmth seemed not only to touch his skin but also his own heart. Kinley closed his eyes and reach out to grope the heart. He felt every inch of it and he memorized it, it was the most beautiful thing that he had ever laid his hands on. Kinley's heart was light; his stomach felt as if he had swallowed one of the fluttery creatures that he had seen flying around the lit skies of Arathia.

"Kinley..." the voice said, "Kinley... Kinley wake up." The voice had changed; Kinley could still feel the heat from The Crystal Heart lingering in his hands, he could also feel cold water on his forehead. Repeatedly it sprinkled, as the woman's voice repeated his name.

"Kinley, wake up."

"He's burning up." Another voice said, a man's voice, gruff and sounding ancient.

Kinley tried to open his eyes, but they seemed to have been glued shut, he tried to lift his arms to pry them open but they were weighted down. Kinley tried to make a sound, but like his eyes, his mouth wouldn't open.

"How far are we from the Trading Post?" the first voice asked, Kinley could now distinguish Enat's voice.

The second voice, he realized, was the voice of Esras, the healer of the tribe, but why was Kinley in his tent? "We are about half way there now, but with the Ree-Kyae so close to us, it shouldn't take us that long to get there."

With no other options, Kinley stayed where he was, listening to the conversation that was going on between Enat and Esras.

"Is there anything you can do for him right now, any way to wake him up?" Enat asked.

"No, nothing, not until the Trading Post anyway, once we are there I may be able to get some herbs potent enough, but until then if he wants to wake up, he has to do it on his own."

Enat had a slight tone of irritation now, "So he is just going to lay there, completely unconscious, possibly to die?"

"No," Esras said, "He is going to lay with you, and I'll talk to the dust when you leave, it'll tell me if he will be okay or not."

The dust that Esras was speaking of was the golden dust of the Man-God. According to legend, the Man-God ripped The Crystal Heart out of his chest and placed it on some mountain. After he did that he died and his body turned to golden dust. Each healer, storyteller, and leader kept a pouch with him or her at all times.

The healers kept the dust to consult; if the right questions are asked the dust can tell them little things about the future. With the leaders, the dust can guide them on the right path for the people; it can also show them the right direction to go. The storytellers use the dust to illumistrate their stories for the council. Kinley felt himself rise from the ground; he was being carried back to Keeva's tent.

Maybe I'll be able to hear what they were talking about earlier, Kinley thought hopefully. That wasn't the case though; Kinley was asleep before they were even half way to Keeva's tent.

*   *   *

Enat and Esras set Kinley down on the dirt floor of the tent. Enat thanked Esras for his help and ushered him out of the tent. She wanted to talk to Keeva privately. Earlier, Enat had woken up from a deep sleep sweating. All she said to Keeva was that Kinley was in trouble and that they had to go. Without question, Keeva followed her out to the river and found Kinley lying on the bank covered in sweat.

Keeva and Enat picked Kinley up and took him to Esras. Keeva had gone back to her tent and waited patiently for Enat and now that she was back Keeva's patience was no longer existent.

"So, what is going on?" Keeva asked.

"Calm down, I'll tell you everything, just give me a chance to breathe." Enat replied.

She leaned against one of the support poles and closed her eyes, breathing in and out. Enat had seen many different things since the dreams had started, but nothing as disturbing as what she had seen in her last dream. She opened her mouth and began telling Keeva how she knew about Kinley. "You know that I have been having these dreams, the ones with the voice. Well in the dream, Kinley was swimming in the river. Arissa was on the shore, looking out over him and you and I were nowhere in sight. The current of the river picked up and Kinley started getting drug along, not able to change his course. Kinley was sucked under the water and then there was a bright flash. The world was light again, like when The Crystal Heart was suspended on the mountain."

Enat waited for a moment, catching her breath and opening her eyes. She looked at Keeva and continued, "Arissa was no longer on the bank of the river you were in her place. I was there, but I was floating over the scene observing. Kinley's head broke the surface of the water and I saw a big green fish dart toward him. It bit down on his arm and the current seemed to push him to shore. You bent down and pulled him out of the water, and then you looked directly at me and spoke; however, your voice wasn't yours you had a man's voice, which was smooth and gentle. You told me that I needed to go to him, you told me that if I didn't he would be left there and all hope would be lost. Then I woke up and you know the rest."

Keeva looked alarmed "Did… did the voice that came out of my mouth… was it the one from your other dreams?"

"Yes, Keeva, it was the same voice. The same

voice that told me the light is coming back, the same voice that told me that the Ree-Kyae's time was short, and the same voice that has been in my dreams for a while now."

"Who do you think it is?" Keeva asked.

Enat thought for a while, she didn't want to sound crazy when she said this but she was sure of whom it was. "Keeva, I don't know how to say this. I have thought long and hard trying to figure out who it could be. At first, I thought it was Kinley's father, but that man never did anything good in life, and there is no way I can imagine him doing anything useful in death.

Keeva noticed that Enat was rubbing her hand over her arm as she usually did when she was nervous. Enat looked over to Kinley, sleeping soundly, her eyes focused on him; Keeva cleared her throat.

Enats head snapped up "Keeva, do not think I am crazy when I say this, but I think that the voice in my dreams... I think it's the voice of the Man-God... I think it is The Crystal Heart."

Chapter Three

The Second Shard

Everyone had woken up and started moving on. Arissa felt horrible about her fight with Kinley. She was doing what she was supposed to, staying up front with the rest of the children. She had been tempted to make her way to the back of the group merging in with the women, then back to the men, where Kinley was. Every time she thought about moving back in line, she remembered the look on Kinley's face.

He had raised valid points about the fishing and walking with the rest who were prepared to fight, but something about the way he spoke the strange shard of rock bugged her. *This thing is not natural* is all that she could remember thinking when Kinley showed it to her. Arissa continued to walk, and continued to think until she convinced herself that she was going to move to the back of the parade of people and confront Kinley. Arissa didn't even try to surreptitiously slide past the people of the tribe; she strode past everyone, her head held high and an intense look on her face.

Inwardly she willed someone to try to stop her; she was determined to make it to Kinley and wanted to fight. Arissa moved past the women to the back where the men were keeping an eye out for the Ree-Kyae. The wind switched and the scent of festering flesh filled her nose. Arissa searched around for Kinley but he was nowhere to be seen.

She did find the boulder man; Arissa learned from the other girls that his name was Peadar. He stood in her way and she wasn't too happy about that. A primal growl eased from her throat and Peadar was surprised. "Don't mess with me right now." was all that she said. Peadar stood there, dumbfounded, and Arissa pushed past him, searching the rest of the group.

Arissa walked around the group three times before she realized that Kinley wasn't present.

Who would know where he was she thought to herself, the answer came with ease *Enat! Of all people, he wouldn't go anywhere without telling his mother?*

Arissa left the group of men and plunged head first into the women, searching out, Enat. She wasn't able to find her there either.

What is going on? She asked herself, *where is everybody?* Finally, she ran straight into Keeva.

"Hey!" Keeva exclaimed annoyed. She turned and saw who had bumped her and her face immediately softened.

"Keeva, have you seen Kinley? I can't find him

anywhere." Arissa's stomach was in knots.

"He and Enat are up front with Esras, but you probably shouldn't go up there just yet." Keeva said not wanting to tell Arissa what was going on.

"Esras? What did that moron do now?" she asked. Hearing that Kinley was with the healer had surprised her, but not as much as it should have. She walked along with Keeva, sending out unanswered probing questions until she gave up. Keeva was very good at keeping things from people.

Arissa drifted off from her and started back towards the front of the procession. There was a certain order to the layout of the nomadic caravan. At the very front of the line was Fallyn, with his torch. Behind him were the council members, followed by the storyteller, Caedmon. Behind Caedmon was the healer, Esras, and then the carts with the "tribe possessions" on them. After that were the personal carts and then the people started with the children, who were arranged by general age, followed by the women and finally the men. This was the set up for a potential battle with the Ree-Kyae, which happened to be their current situation.

Arissa had made it through the group of women and children, but found herself having issues slyly making her way through the carts. Her feet kept being run over by the big wheels.

Eventually she made it up to Esras' cart. It was covered, which meant that someone was inside. Esras was walking beside the cart, making sure that the two people pulling it weren't hitting any unnecessary bumps in the road.

Esras looked over at her, "Can I help you?" he asked.

"Is that Kinley in your cart?" she asked out of breath from battling the mob behind them.

"Arissa, Enat asked me to watch for you, and informed that you were allowed in."

"Yes, but… what happened?" she asked.

"Enat and Keeva came to me carrying Kinley. They said that he went out to get some fish before heading back to the end of the line. He was bitten by one of the fish in the river." Arissa's head instantly filled with horrible images of appendages bitten off, scars all over his torso, and many of the monstrous creatures the river had birthed.

"Arissa, Kinley has been poisoned. The fish that bit him was toxic."

Arissa stopped dead in her tracks the people pulling the cart behind them ran into her. She didn't apologize for stopping in the middle of the path, instead she ran to catch up to Esras' cart. She grabbed hold of the pole on the front of the cart, and with a great amount of agility, she swung herself into it. Inside, hung two glow-grub bottles dimly casting their soft light throughout the cart. There were piles of boxes, different concoctions of scales, skin and reconstituted plants used in the creating of medicine. Viscous liquids bubbled away over small fires; they put off an acrid smell.

This is surely a place of magic, Arissa thought to herself. She noticed a lump on the floor; it looked almost like a pile of blankets. Arissa scanned the pile and noticed a woman lying next to it, asleep.

"Enat?" Arissa shouted unknowingly. The woman sat bolt upright, but there was no surprise on her face. Enat seemed to have a different aura to her, strong, defiant and determined; this was not something that Arissa was used to.

Enat had always seemed weak and helpless, someone that needed somebody else to do everything for her. This look in her eyes made her almost unrecognizable.

A cool, steely voice flowed out of her throat "Arissa, can I help you?"

oh no, thought Arissa, *she blames me for what happened to him.*

"Is he alright?" was all she spoke aloud.

"He will be," Enat replied, "Esras spoke to the dust before we left, he said that, according to the dust, Kinley has a much bigger part in this world than any of us realize. He said that Kinley was going to be even better than he had been before he was poisoned."

Arissa didn't know what to say to that, she just wanted to see him. She knelt down beside him, reaching for the blankets that covered his face in the dimly lit cart. Enats eyes didn't leave Arissa's hands as she reached towards Kinley, and she noticed this. For the first time since she had been a small child, Arissa was afraid of Enat. Still, nothing was said or done to prevent Arissa from moving the blankets down, so she continued. Kinleys face had changed, his jaw line was more pronounced, beads of sweat rolled off his forehead. His cheekbones had risen a little higher; slight changes that made her best friend look like a stranger.

"What's happening to him?" Arissa asked. She wasn't necessarily talking to Enat, but she answered anyway.

"The poison is changing him. Like the dust told Esras, he will be better than he was before he was poisoned."

"There was nothing wrong with him before though." Arissa stated.

"That's true, but Kinley is going to face trials and tribulations in his life, he is going to have to give up a lot, he needs to be ready for that, as do you Arissa."

Arissa was surprised, she hadn't thought about that before. *What would happen if something does happen to Kinley? What would I do if he didn't want to speak to me anymore? Would sI accept it, or would I tell him that he didn't have a choice, and that I was stuck to him in our symbiotic relationship.*

Arissa looked up at Enat; her eyes had softened a little bit. "Arissa, I know how you feel about my son, but if you want to continue to be in his life you have to realize how he feels about you. You are Kinleys friend. His best friend, but you will never have his heart. He is special; ever since he was born his heart has belonged to someone else."

Arissa was instantly embarrassed. She thought she was able to hide how she felt from Enat; obviously, she was more observant than Arissa had given her credit.

"Arissa, I know that you love him, but the question is can you love him in the way that he wants you to love him?" Arissa looked down, not saying anything. Her heart was breaking into a thousand pieces in her chest.

"If that's the only way I can love him," she said, "then I don't have a choice, do I?" A tear slid down her cheek, only one, and she didn't let Enat see it, it was wiped away while it was still rolling down and before it reached her lips.

Arissa stayed by Kinleys side, there were times

when she could swear that he was able to hear her. He never moved, he was always still and Enat constantly watched over him, aware of every slight movement and every sound. Arissa wanted to be alone with him, but that never happened, Enat was always by his side, meals were brought in and progress was made towards the Varian Trading Post.

Arissa would whisper her apologies to him, she told him he was right about the fishing, and she told him that he was right about her staying up front, but she found herself apologizing most for the shard. She apologized for making him throw it away, and for not understanding how much he cared for it, she apologized for letting such a trivial thing cause damage to their friendship. It seemed that she had been apologizing for more than half of what was left of their journey to the Trading Post when she finally fell asleep.

*   *   *

Kinley had spent a long time drifting in and out of sleep. Changing constantly, he could feel things re-arranging when he was lucid, but while he was sleeping, he was oblivious to everything.

He felt his bone structure change, he could feel his muscles tense and relax over and over again he was physically exhausted, as if he had been doing hard labor since he was bitten. His hair grew long extremely fast; light brown curls had replaced his straight dark brown hair. His teeth constantly tingled, not knowing why, he was afraid that they were getting sharp and pointed like the Ree-Kyae teeth. Was it possible that the fish bite was turning him into one of them? Was he somehow mutating into one of those evil and disgusting creatures?

He was unable to open his eyes, and still unable to move, so he had no idea what he even looked like. He could hear the voices though. They were more easily recognizable now, His mother was there but there was something different about her voice, she sounded fierce, not as he had ever heard her before. Esras came in occasionally to check on him. He could feel Esras cold hand on his neck and wrists. Keeva came in once and a while to check on Enat, to make sure that Esras was right when he was reading the dust and that Kinley was okay.

There was another voice there as well, Arissa, she had come, what seemed like forever ago. He wasn't awake when she did, but was a little bit after, when she had seemed to be apologizing for everything that she had ever said or done to him. She promised him that if he woke up, she wouldn't do anything to upset him ever again. Kinley knew that factor was completely unrealistic and out of her control, but he was unable to object.

He found himself wanting to fall into his dreams more often. He could walk there, he could talk there, everything that he couldn't do in his mother's world he could do in his dream world. He couldn't make himself go visit it though; he had to be called into it by the voice. He became friends with this voice; it showed him times when The Crystal Heart was whole, it let him know where the Ree-Kyae were, and that his family and friends were safe for now. It even told him how he would wake up, but not when.

"It will be painful Kinley, you will feel a

stabbing pain in your chest, when you wake up. There is going to be blood, and a lot of it, but don't worry, by the time you wake the wound will already have closed up. No scars will be present." The voice said.

"What's going to happen to me?" Kinley asked.

"I am going to enter you again." the voice replied smoothly.

"Who are you?" Kinley asked the voice again, he kept getting the same answer but he couldn't see how that was possible. With patience, the voice gave the same answer "I am you, and you are me. We are one and the same."

"That's what you have been saying, how are you me when I have never heard from you before?"

"I have known you since the womb, I was with you through puberty, I will be with you when your mother and friends return to the ground and I will be with you until you find your place in the dirt. When you die, you will be with me. You and I are together Kinley, always, my heart belongs to you, and yours to me. Fate has bound us."

"You said that you will enter me again, should I be asking the question, what are you instead of who are you?" Kinley asked.

"No, I am a person, you may think of me as a what, but I am a who."

The scene in front of his face changed into something that he had done before. He could see himself sitting on a petrified tree. Nothing came out of his mouth as he stood up and began walking along the river. The Kinley in the scene looked down and kicked at something, it was the rock, his rock. He picked it up and looked at it, pressed his finger to it.

"I know this," Kinley said, "this is where I found my rock, but what does that have to do with you?"

"Kinley, that rock wasn't a rock, that rock is me, that rock is very special, that rock is one of the shards of The Crystal Heart."

*   *   *

Time passed as Kinley lay motionless; Arissa sat next to him dealing with her own internal struggle. It seemed to Arissa that his face changed daily. Little changes, like the shape of his eyes, length of his eyelashes and the downturn of his mouth. There were some big changes too, his skin got a little bit darker, and his hair grew long, and curly, very fast. He had built muscle while he was sleeping. His body shape now resembled Peadar, strong and solid, but not as big, he still had a strange delicate way about him.

Arissa brushed the hair out of his face, he was still sweating, and that's something else that hadn't changed. She had taken to wiping his brow, chest, arms and legs with a moist cloth to keep him clean. Enat was sleeping next to Kinley now. She had mostly stayed around the cart leaving the inside occasionally, to stretch her legs. Keeva checked in with them, she and Enat would sometimes walk together outside the cart, talking, Arissa didn't know what about, she assumed that it was idle gossip.

Enat woke from her dream and sat up. She tried to sound calm but there was a note of urgency in her voice. "Arissa!" she exclaimed, "You should go for a walk. Stretch your legs a bit." Arissa didn't want to leave but she could tell by the look in Enats eyes that there was no room for argument. She moved the flap with her hand, grabbed hold of the pole at the front of the cart again, and swung down, when she hit the ground her knees locked and she tumbled forward into a summersault. She hadn't expected the cart to be moving, spending so much time in it made the movement seem like stillness. She felt pain in her hand and looked down. There was a rock splintered in deeply, almost through her hand it was relatively long, about the size of her little finger.

It looked like it was made of the same material as the one Kinley had found.

This is it, she thought to herself, *this is how I can finally apologize to Kinley for making him throw his rock away, I'll replace it with this one.*

She pulled it out of her hand with one swift movement, like removing a large splinter. It looked almost exactly like Kinleys rock, definitely the same material, just a little shorter than Kinley's, and this one didn't have the black and grey rounded end on it; instead, this rock was completely smooth. It had penetrated her skin at an angle starting at the heel of her palm and going up towards her ring finger.

This is weird, thought Arissa, *it looks like this was part of something bigger, something sculpted.* She looked down at her palm, which was still bloody. She wiped the blood away and saw that the wound had already healed.

She held the rock in her hand until she was able to find a place for it. She remembered how easily the one that Kinley found had sliced through flesh and how he kept it wrapped in leather. She searched the unattended carts rolling past her until she was able to find some. Since all the animals were dead, leather was rare, and Arissa had none of her own. She took a piece from one of the carts and stuck the rock in the center of it; she wrapped it up into a neat little package and then tied it off with a piece of fiber she found. She did just as Kinley did with it and stuck it in her back pocket, hoping that the rock wouldn't slice through the leather and dig into her skin.

Arissa walked around a little bit to do as Enat asked, as well as to test the strength of the leather in her back pocket. After that, she swung back up onto the cart and under the cover in one agile and fluid movement. She walked over to Kinley and sat next to him.

"How was your walk?" Enat asked. She hadn't spoken to Arissa much since she got there, and her voice still had a steely tone to it, but Arissa was thankful for the conversation.

"It was fine, my legs are all stretched. Thanks. Is he still the same." Arissa replied.

"Yes, he is still the same, for some reason I think he'll be awake soon though, let's call it mother's intuition." Enat said, lying back down beside Kinley, "Let's get some sleep now."

Arissa obeyed lying down next to Kinley; she looked at his face, wearing the same expression it had been when she first got to him. Her eyelids felt heavy, and she allowed them to close, his face being the last thing that she saw before she fell asleep.

*   *   *

"Arissa? What are you doing here?" Kinley was in her dream; this didn't surprise her considering that his face was the last thing she saw before she fell asleep. Arissa ran to Kinley and pulled him into a hug, whether it was a dream or not, she was happy to have Kinley in her arms.

"I am so worried about you right now. You are just lying there asleep." She told him. *This dream is different,* Arissa thought, *I can actually control what I say and do in it.*

"Don't worry about me," Kinley told her, "I have something I have to tell you. I heard all of your apologies to me, and I am sorry too I…"Kinley started but Arissa interrupted him before he could get to his point.

"You are sorry for what? There is no reason for you to be sorry."

"Arissa, will you please just listen to me?" Kinley said. Her reply was short; "Yes." and she held her tongue.

"Arissa, I lied to you, I didn't throw away my rock. It's in my back pocket wrapped in the leather scrap."

"You lied to me? How could you lie to me? Kinley you said that you threw it away, I watched you drop that thing…"

Kinley interrupted her this time, "It's a good thing I didn't throw it away. Arissa, that rock is a piece of The Crystal Heart."

It seemed impossible to Kinley, but Arissa's face actually got whiter. Only her skin was no longer moonlight white, it was more of a sickly white and there was no shine to it at all.

"It's… What…?" she managed to get out.

"It's a piece of The Crystal Heart. I couldn't tell you this before but it has been in my dreams, each time I have slept, I heard a voice. It was a man's voice, very gentle and warm… do you remember when I woke up and you were packing up our stuff?"

Arissa nodded and Kinley continued with his confession, "That was the first time I had heard the voice. It kept telling me that he and I were the same person, this whole time he has been telling me that there is something I have to do, I don't know what it is yet, but I am getting closer to finding out."

"Yeah, well, did he tell you something useful? Like how you are going to wake up from this coma, for instance."

"Yes," Kinley said with a warm smile, "basically I am going to have to die to wake up."

Arissa's heart sunk, "You are going to have to die, to wake up? That doesn't make sense Kinley."

"It does when it's explained to you; you have to kill me Arissa." Kinley said calmly, as if he had practiced saying this repeatedly.

"I… have… to… WHAT?" Arissa looked at him stupidly. She started hyperventilating and sat down putting her head between her knees. Once her breath was recovered she looked up at Kinley, he stood there, looking like the same Kinley she had known, none of the physical changes that had taken place outside of the dream world were reflected in this mental image.

It's ok, this is only a dream, and I don't really have to kill him.

Suddenly there was another voice in her head, not just her own. It was rich and smooth, full and supple, commanding yet meek all at the same time.

Arissa, you have to do this. This is not a dream, you found a piece of me today, and I brought you here, wake us up Arissa, give us life.

Arissa blinked and looked around. *You are… you're… The Crystal Heart?* She asked.

Yes, and this is your destiny Arissa, you must wake us up.

"Wow, Kinley, you look like you used to." Arissa said, not showing that she had heard the voice. "You look so different now, the same, but different."

"I have been preparing, my love has told me that I am going to be doing something great and dangerous. He said that he was going to change me. Make me into what it takes to complete the task at hand, I have been able to feel the changes, but not to see them I have been able to hear you, but not to see you, same thing with Ma, I have been able to hear her, but not to see her. Arissa, I need to wake up, will you please wake us up? I'll tell you what you have to do."

Arissa still wasn't convinced that she wasn't entirely dreaming, this one felt so real and has been the only one in which was able to control herself.

She paused for a moment and looked around, her jaw dropped in shock. The scenery here was completely different from in any other dream that she had ever had. This world was bright and beautiful, like nothing she had ever fully imagined. She had dreams of the world Enat and Keeva lived in, but this was different, it was vibrant and real somehow.

She could touch things, and feel them on her skin, as opposed to just dreaming that she felt them. There was lush green moss covering the ground under her feet and she felt its spring as she shifted her weight from the back of her feet to the front. She felt the heat radiating off her skin and a cool breeze as well. She saw life all around her, animals, some as small as her fist, some larger than the carts that the people of the tribe used to carry their supplies.

"What is this?" She asked to no one, and she hadn't expected to get an answer back, especially not one back from two people at once, the voice spoke in her head, and through Kinley's mouth at the same time

"This is my world, or rather an echo of it, memories if you will. I have shown Kinley my world extensively. His skin has touched me and life is running free here. Kinley is learning many valuable lessons, ones that will help him in his task. I have to send you back soon, you must wake us up it is your destiny."

Arissa didn't want to leave this world, it was beautiful, and everything that hers wasn't, there was no fear of the Ree-Kyae anywhere, everything lived together and the only violence was what supported life.

"So, now I have to tell you how to wake us up." Kinley said. "Take my shard out of my pocket, unwrap it and slide off the sheath, and plunge it into my chest, as deep as it will go. This will scare you because I will die before I wake."

Arissa shuddered. "You have to make sure you hit my heart, don't second guess yourself; if you do, you will over think what you have to do and miss. My blood will bubble up out of the wound around the shard, but you have to leave it in there, pull it out only when I stop breathing, if you pull it out before I am dead, it will heal up, but I won't wake. Don't be afraid, Arissa, You're my best friend, and I need you."

"What if… what if I can't do it?" she stuttered looking down, as if she was afraid to meet his eyes.

"You are the strongest person I know, the only one that I think could do it, it's why I didn't ask Ma, and why I waited for you. Do you remember when boulder guy…"Kinley said, interrupted by Arissa, "Peadar, his name is Peadar."

"Sorry," Kinley corrected, "do you remember when Peadar came up to you and told you that you would be a distraction if the Ree-Kyae attacked. I played along because I didn't want to make trouble, the truth is that I think you could kill more Ree-Kyae then Peadar and I combined. My love and I think that you are the perfect person to do this, you are strong and sensitive and you care about me too much to deviate from the directions. I trust this task to you, and I think that you will do perfectly at it."

Arissa smiled at him, it didn't reach her eyes, but it wasn't a fake smile, it was a worried smile.

"So stab you in the heart with a shard of The Crystal Heart, wait until you are completely dead and then remove it? You are sure you will make it back?"

Kinley smiled at her, "Yes and yes, I will be okay as long as you do this. My time is short in my loves memories, you have to go now, wait until the next stop to wake me up, but no sooner, okay?"

"Next stop," she said, "I got it." She pulled Kinley into a hug, and kissed him on his cheek. With Kinley in her arms, the scene faded to a blinding light and no dream picked up where that one left off.

*　　*　　*

Arissa slept for a long time; right after she decided to lie down next to Kinley and her eyes were closed. Enat sat up and watched. Enat knew what was coming, she had known since she found Kinley by the water that Arissa was going to kill him. She had been told this by the voice in her dream, and though she knew that it was the only way to wake him up, she told no one. Not Esras while he was looking over Kinley, not Keeva when she had asked for the story, and not even Arissa who was going to be the one to kill him. She tried not to be angry with Arissa for what she was going to do, but she couldn't help it.

Arissa was going to hurt her son, and every instinct in the core of her body told her not to let it happen, but the voice had been right about everything else, and though her son may look different, Kinley was still Kinley, and she wanted him back. Earlier, while she was sleeping, the voice told her to send Arissa away, it told her that Kinley was going to be able to hear her and that she needed to tell him about her dreams, so she did. Arissa went out to stretch her legs and Enat told Kinley everything, told him about the voice, told him about the task that the voice said was going to happen. She told him about the world she saw and the animals, she told him about the plants and she assured him that it was all coming back. She held his sweat-laden head in her hands, running her palm over his forehead; she sung one of the old songs to him, hoping that it would reach him wherever he was. Then she set his head back down and Arissa swung into the covered cart.

Moment after moment they were getting closer to stopping, Arissa had woken up, fully rested and feeling better then she had in a long time, but something was weighing on her mind. She was trying to decide if the dream that she had was actually a dream or some sort of out of body experience.

"How did you sleep?" Enat asked coldly. *This*

is really affecting her differently than I thought it would.

"I slept well, how about you?" She asked Enat.

"I slept… okay, I guess."

"Enat, how far are we from the next stopping point?"

"Well, the Ree-Kyae seem to be backing off and we are still about three quarters of the way out from the Trading Post, so I would say that we have one or two stops left in between, it depends on what Fallyn reads from the dust. Probably pretty close, and before you ask, nothing has changed with Kinley." Her eyes fixed on her son while she spoke, they started to swell with tears, but she was not going to cry.

She had noticed a change in herself, when Kinley was bitten and she found out that he was going to die, she became her old self, back before Kinley's father had raped her. That broke her, but now she was strong again, she was able to feel something other than sadness. Kinley had always been her rose among weeds, she saw very little of that same person in him, now that he had changed so much she couldn't see anything of his father in him.

"Okay," Arissa said, "thanks Enat. For what it's worth I am sorry about Kinley." For the first time since she found Kinley Enat looked at Arissa and saw her as Kinley's friend not as a murderer. She was the little girl that had grown up with Kinley, the one that had the crush and brought him some dead thistles, the little girl who would dress up as a Ree-Kyae with mud on her skin in place of sores, and chase Kinley around the camp.

She was the little girl who Kinley went to whenever there was a problem or some exciting news, and it was then that Enat knew that she wouldn't kill

Kinley if she didn't think it was going to work. Arissa trusts Kinley with her life and this shows that he does the same. For the first time since she had found Kinley, she was at peace with the situation.

Arissa needed some time to think, so she decided she was going to walk with the children. She swung down from the cart and walked in the group. She had grown up with all of these people throughout her years, but really knew none of them; she hadn't realized how close she had been to Kinley until she had to kill him. Her best friend, that was an understatement, he was her only friend.

She hadn't become obsessed with the idle gossip that other girls her age had, she hadn't ever liked trying on others clothing she would rather wrestle or throw clumps of dry dirt at others. She didn't look the part, but she was rough and strong, as Kinley had told her in her dream. She could probably take out more Ree-Kyae then Peadar could. Though he was built bigger than she was he lacked her speed and agility. It was this reason that Arissa had started drifting to the back of the group. When she reached the group of men, Peadar saw her and strode over to her.

"What do you want?" Arissa asked, her voice lacking any fear and full of confrontational confidence. Peadar looked over at her; Arissa knew just what he was going to say.

"You again? You know you shouldn't be back here, if something happens…"

Arissa interrupted him "then I'll be the one saving your butt."

"*You*?" Peadar bellowed a laugh. "*You* are going to save *me*?

Arissa didn't like where this was going. "Yeah, I guess you're right," she said feigning delicacy, "I mean, you are so… big and strong, and I am just a girl."

"Uh… yeah...," he said trying to choose his next words carefully, "let's go ahead and get you back up front."

He reached his hand out and put it on Arissa's shoulder; she grabbed his arm and swung herself behind him. Peadar was stunned and Arissa took advantage of it. She kicked his mid back with the heel of her foot knocking him to the ground, face first. She saw a stick by his head and picked it up thrusting it to the base of his head, the stick snapped with the pressure, and like she wanted, didn't penetrate the skin; if had been a knife it would have gone right under the back of the skull and into the brain also severing the spinal cord. The stick was still pressed to his neck and Arissa had a big smile on her face.

"Now, can we get over all this macho man bullshit and just let me fight with the rest of the fighters. I know that you are at least one man short with Kinley gone, and I can take his place until he is well again."

Arissa stood up, making sure to put a little pressure on the knee currently residing in his back. His spine popped and Arissa grabbed his hand and pulled him up from the ground. Peadar's face was blank, no amusement or surprise showed on his face, just like the impression Kinley got, Arissa could tell that Peadar didn't like to be corrected… or proven wrong.

"Fine," Peadar said, "you can stay back here, and you can fight, but if the Ree-Kyae decide that they want to attack us, don't expect any of us to protect you." Arissa smiled, this time she tried to make her face mimic Enats new expression of cold unbridled strength.

"I've said it before; I'll be the one saving you."

There was no armor suited for a female, so she had to have some made, meaning that she had some time before she would be allowed at the back of the group for good. She received looks from the women of the nomadic tribe, some were glairs others were full of admiration. Fallyn had been very proud to break tradition and allow a woman to fight.

"Never before has a women been allowed to join the men in battle. I am pleased with your decision and with your desire to defend your people, Arissa, and I will tell you this now. If you hadn't taken Peadar down, you would still be walking ahead with the children, and if you had tried and failed, you would probably be riding in Esras' cart, and not of your own free will."

Caedmon had started fallowing Arissa around not wanting to miss anything she did; he was putting a story together of the first female fighter and was planning to unveil it at the Trading Post to the other storytellers. It was hard for the old man to get around; he walked with a long pointed rod, limping on his left leg. Arissa and Kinley listened to one of his stories on how he was injured. Caedmon had been a fighter once and one of the Ree-Kyae had done some permanent damage to his calf, forcing him to limp around for the rest of his life. He gave up fighting and started to pick up storytelling.

He trained with one of the greatest, but soon surpassed his master in the field of illumination and was now not only known by every storyteller, but also every healer, leader and most Varians in Arathia. It was an honor to have a story told about you, it was an even greater honor for Caedmon to create your story, but still, it was annoying to be followed around by an old man, limping with his walking stick and yelling "Girl, wait up. Arissa, I can't move that fast. My old bones ache, lets rest for a moment." Even worse, Fallyn had declared that they were going to stop soon and she was supposed to kill Kinley, she couldn't do that with Caedmon watching, she would have no way to explain what she was doing, or why she was doing it.

She was walking to her fitting for her armor Caedmon behind her chanting his usual girl-wait-ups and you're-making-this-difficult-for-me's when Peadar came up behind her. He turned to look at Caedmon "Get lost old man." He said.

Arissa just stared at him, how he could talk to Caedmon like that, with such disrespect. Not only that, but Caedmon was a much respected member of their nomadic tribe and a celebrity among storytellers. Arissa wanted to take him down again but Caedmon just looked at him, a bright smile on his face.

"Old man? Peadar, this is how you talk to me now? It used to be Grandpa tell me why you limp again, grandpa tell me about The Crystal Heart. Now it's get lost old man?"

Arissa looked at Caedmon stunned, *a grandson* she thought *I didn't know Caedmon had any family and his grandson is Peadar, the boulder man?*

This seemed impossible, but sure enough, Peadar walked over to his limping grandfather and carefully gave him a hug.

"How have you been gramps?" the old man smiled a smile that reached his eyes, one could tell that he was definitely proud of his grandson.

"I've been better; the ole leg is giving me some trouble. You know, trying to keep up with the she-fighter isn't helping to much either. Here you think she would be more patient with *me* trying to create a story about her and all. You'd think that she would appreciate it more."

Oh great, she thought, *they are just alike, they both think they are the greatest thing in Arathia.* Arissa rolled her eyes and continued walking to the moving cart where her armor was being made.

Peadar hugged his grandfather, whispered something in his ear and then started walking towards Arissa. Surprisingly Caedmon didn't fallow.

"Girl… Arissa, slow down I want to talk to you." He said, the slip up almost earning him a balled up fist to the face. Arissa slowed down, but only slightly. Peadar caught up with her in only a few strides. "So… uh… hi." He said. "Uh… hi." Arissa replied with attitude seeping from between her lips, still walking to the cart. He looked down as he walked.

"What did you want to talk to me about?" Arissa sounded annoyed.

"Listen, I was just thinking, when we stop, if you wouldn't mind, you know, coming over to my family's fire and sharing a meal with us. It's just my grandpa and I, and the company would be nice."

Arissa thought, *now the old man has his grandson trying to make me come over so he can question me more. Honestly!*

Arissa had started getting irritated; she didn't think she had accomplished anything worth a story, let alone a story from Caedmon. A plan started forming in her head.

"That depends on whose cooking?" Arissa said, the probing question meaning a lot more to her then to Peadar.

"Well Gramps I guess, he always cooks when we stop, except when he has a council meeting." That's exactly what she wanted to hear.

"I'll make you a deal, you keep him off my back for a little while, from now until after we stop and I'll share a meal with you. How's that?" Arissa was extremely pleased with herself. She had figured out a way to keep Caedmon away while she killed Kinley.

"Sounds good, Gramps is a stubborn old codger but I'll see what I can do, and Arissa, thank you."

Arissa was amazed at the change in Peadar's attitude; the normally chauvinistic very rude big brute of a man had softened a little, at least towards her. As she watched him walk away, he shoved one of the other fighters out of the way and tripped one just a little bit after.

He may be a jerk, but he has a very cute butt. Arissa smiled as she swung herself up on the cart where her armor was being made. Luckily, the woman making it was one of the women who thought that Arissa was a trailblazer and not one of the ones who were afraid that letting her fight would distract the men.

"Hello Arissa, sorry this isn't done yet, its difficult pounding the ancient leather with the metal, these materials are very rare you know, hopefully they protect you in case we do get attacked."

"Yes, hopefully, I am sure they will, you're work is beautiful." Arissa said.

"Let's try on the breast plate next; it's the one that I have been working on the most, and it's also the last piece that needs to be completed."

Arissa tried on the breastplate, pointing out which spots pinched and where it was to loose and then the woman making it, Arissa hadn't bothered to commit her name to memory, began pounding at it with a hammer. She dismissed Arissa after having her try it on a few more times. The last time all the spots that Arissa had pointed out were fingered and measured so the woman could see how much distance was where, or how much more it needed to be pounded in.

Arissa left her cart and headed towards Esras medicine cart, she was tired and she still wasn't sleeping in her own cart. They had been walking for a long time now, not stopping, this is what people were doing, half would sleep while the other half walked and transported.

Arissa swung up into the covered area of the cart and took up her usual space next to Kinley. Enat was already asleep on the other side of him, but that didn't stop her from telling him everything that went on since she had last seen him. She left out one detail, and that was her shard of The Crystal Heart, the one wrapped in leather in her back pocket, that she was touching. Arissa was still talking, her eyes closed, as she drifted to sleep. There were no weird dreams, no voices, there was no Kinley and no Crystal Heart, there was just light this time, beautiful white light.

Chapter Four

Waking up

Everyone in the tribe was getting irritated very quickly. They had been walking for a very long time, their stomachs growling due to a lack of time for fishing. All the reserve had been eaten while they were walking. Fallyn had a choice to make, the dust had told him if they stopped that the Ree-Kyae would have a greater chance of catching up, but with no food and very little patience left among the tribe, Fallyn had no other choice.

It would have to be a very fast stop as well as the only stop until they get to the Trading Post. The Ree-Kyae are always outnumbered at the Trading Post and making these tough decisions are what the leaders of the tribes do. They would walk a little more, and then they would stop, stock up on food, boil water, possibly get some rest, and then head back towards the Trading Post. Fallyn left his position at the head of the line and moved towards the back, where the fighters were.

"Men," Fallyn started, "and Arissa, we are going to be stopping soon. I need all of you here, and on your guard. According to the dust, we are still not in the clear but we are out of food, almost out of water, and legs are getting tired. It's a difficult decision, but it's my decision."

"Fallyn, Arissa still doesn't have her armor." Peadar said smugly.

Arissa shot him a glare then spoke up for herself. "It's almost done, I don't think there will be a problem, and I should have it pretty quickly."

"She shouldn't even be back here yet, if the Ree-Kyae came at us and she didn't have her armor she would be susceptible to anything they threw at her."

"Arissa, Peadar raises a very valid point. We need everyone, but we need everyone who has a possibility of being here after a battle as well as before." Fallyn had seemed to make his decision. "Arissa I want you to stay closer to the front, at least until you get your armor."

Arissa shot another glare at Peadar; her attitude was one of the things that he liked about her. She was unbelievably defiant and very stubborn. She had also been the only person to take him down.

He wondered what her weapon would be, *Kieron was supposed to be meeting with her right after the meeting. I doubt he would give her a bow and arrow and he probably thinks that she is too weak to be able to lift a sword, definitely not a mace or a battle-axe. He had been presented with a new situation, maybe one that would inspire him to make something, a new style of weapon, and keep Arissa out of harm's way for a while longer.*

Maybe he could talk to Kieron, get to him before Arissa, and plant the seed that she needed a new kind of weapon.

I could use Caedmon, he thought, *I could tell Kieron that he is making a story about her, and that she should have a completely new weapon, never before heard of by any Varian.*

Fallyn spoke a little more, not that Peadar really paid attention. As soon as Fallyn dismissed the group, he slipped out before Arissa. He walked forward to the procession of carts which were moving forward, setting the pace for all of the people behind them. The weapon makers cart was relatively close to the back of the procession. Peadar climbed up the side of the moving cart and walked into the covered area. Kieron was sitting on top of a cushion on the floor of the cart. Peadar said nothing; he just came forward and stood in front of Kieron, waiting for him to speak first.

Kieron looked up at Peadar, "I've seen a lot of blood caused by the weapons I create, but all of them have been wielded by the hands of men. This one, I have no clue what this warrior, this woman fighter, needs." Kieron motioned with his hand for Peadar to sit.

"When you walked up to me for the first time, I knew your style, I knew what weapon would be an extension of you, I know nothing about her fighting style, I know not of a weapon that would suit a woman. A woman fighter." Kieron spoke the last three words with a sense of amusement.

Peadar assumed that Kieron wasn't too happy

about Fallyn's decision to allow a woman to fight, let alone making a weapon for her.

"Kieron, I am here for a reason. Arissa, the woman fighter, my grandfather is creating a story about her. I was just thinking that you should make something new, something never before seen."

Kieron grumbled to himself, he was obviously upset about having to make anything for her as it was; now Peadar was here suggesting that he create something completely new.

"Caedmon is creating a new story for the girl?" Kieron asked, and he had started to come around to the idea. "I still don't like making something for *her* bur if Caedmon is going to tell about it, and if she is any good with it, then it should be worth it. I'll need to see how she fights though." Kieron smiled mischievously, "For that I will need a skilled fighter." Kieron looked at Peadar.

"You want me to fight Arissa?"

"Peadar, I want you to make her work, I want to see that she deserves to fight, that she deserves this story your grandfather is creating about her and that she deserves this weapon I may, or may not, be making for her. I don't want to make a weapon for this woman, and have her shame my name in Caedmon's story." Peadar was starting to get annoyed with the old man, but didn't have a chance to show it because just as he was about to speak, Arissa walked in, silently.

"Kieron, how are you doing today?" Arissa asked.

Kieron looked at Peadar and grunted towards Arissa, he allowed a gruff "Fine" to pass his lips. Peadar stood up and turned to face Arissa then began walking over; he put one hand on her shoulder. With an apologetic look in his eye, Peadar swept his foot under Arissa, knocking her on her butt.

Arissa looked up at him, confusion in her eyes. Peadar looked at her, his eyes were fierce and he mouthed the words "fight back". In a split second she propped herself on her arm, and swept her foot under Peadar knocking him down. Without hesitation, she grabbed the hair on the back of his head and slammed his face into the ground.

Peadar was dazed for a moment and before it wore off Arissa was on him, punching, kicking and bruising his body in every way that she could think of. She picked him up and climbed on his shoulders with her legs spread a little bit, she brought both elbows down on each side between his head and her legs, digging deeply into them. Peadar collapsed to his knees. She jumped off him, doing a back flip in the air landing behind him; to take him down she kicked his head launching him to the side.

She looked at Peadar, he was doubled over on the floor clutching at the side of his head that she had kicked with one hand, and his other was around his ribs. Blood was running down his face and teeth were tightly pressed together in an expression of pain and rage.

He really hates being beaten. Arissa thought to herself. It was then that she looked over at Kieron, his mouth hanging wide open. Still sitting on his cushion on the floor of his cart, he looked from her to Peadar repeatedly.

"Peadar, get up, go to get yourself cleaned up, Arissa stay, we need to take some measurements." With that, Peadar limped out of Kieron's cart. Arissa felt the cart stop for a brief moment and then it continued.

"Arissa, I am very, very surprised at your speed and agility." Kieron finally stood up from his place on the floor; he took a string off the shelf and started measuring Arissa. "Which hand do you use more often?" Arissa raised her right hand and Kieron took his string measuring her arm. First, he was measured from shoulder to elbow, then from elbow to wrist.

He bent her arm and measured the distance, straightened the arm and measured the distance. He measured from the base of her palm to the tip of each finger as well as the distance between them when she spread them out. The last thing that he measured was the width of her shoulders.

"I know what I am going to make for you, come back after the next stop; I can't work well with my cart bouncing like this so it may take me a little longer than usual." Arissa left Kieron in his cart, he was busy, back turned to her and leaning over his workbench fiddling with sharp tools and pieces of leather, Arissa assumed that he was putting them in order to get to work on her weapon.

What is Kinley going to think when he finds all this out? She wondered.

*   *   *

They were getting closer and closer to stopping and the anxiety started building in Arissa's chest. At one point she had to stop walking, the group gained some distance on her. She hadn't worked with being at peace with the idea of killing her best friend yet. She had tried thinking of herself as a healer but that didn't work. At one point, she thought that she was just being too pessimistic, that if she thought of it as bringing someone back to life as opposed to killing them it would be easier, but she was wrong, it didn't make it any easier.

This was Kinley, she had grown up with him, how is she going to be able to watch him gasp, watch the blood bubble up in his throat and around the shard, how will she be alright knowing she has done this to him? She imagined seeing the life drain from his eyes and she felt sick. The normal darkness seemed to be even greater, pressing in around her; she could barely see the group up ahead of her. She ran to meet them not wanting them to leave her behind, she was surprised when she finally met them and the fighters were sitting down, stopped and resting.

This is it, Arissa thought as she walked past the fighters catching up to the women. She had a blank stare on her face, she noticed Keeva unpacking her cart up ahead. Enat was with her, *what would Enat say if she knew was I was about to do*. Arissa thought, *She would kill me, of that I am sure*. At that moment Enat looked up and caught her eye, it was full of pain, but not the broken pain that normally sat in Enats eyes, this pain was different, it was a red pain, full of passion. For a moment Arissa thought that Enat knew what she was going to do, and was about to stop her.

Enat started walking over to her; Arissa was starting to get afraid.

"Arissa, hold on." the words that came out of Enats mouth reflected none of the pain inspired rage in her eyes. Arissa stood in place; the dead look still clung to her features.

"I am going to hang back here with Keeva, are you going to Esras cart?" Arissa, still with the blank look on her face, nodded.

"Alright," Enat said, "no one should bother you. Esras already checked on him, right when we stopped." Enat walked back to Keeva and started unloading the equipment and setting up the wine colored tent.

Arissa made her way to Esras cart, she stared at it for a moment, thinking about what she was about to do.

I know this is what he wanted, what he needs. Esras eyed her as she got closer to the cart, but she didn't notice, she was lost in her thoughts. Instead of her usual swinging up to the cart and into the canvas flap that allowed entrance to the covered portion, she climbed up the front, and walked in. She looked down at Kinley, still the same, but he was so different all at once.

He was much more muscular than he had been. His face looked almost the same, she couldn't pretend that he was someone else; really the only difference was that his features were more angular. His jaw line was a little broader, the bridge of his nose now connected to the space between his eyes, his curly hair hung in his eyes, he was tan, and he was beautiful. She felt like she was about to kill an angel, her stomach turned.

She started reaching towards his back pocket, to get out his shard then her hand stopped of its own accord. She couldn't use his shard to kill him. He loved that rock; he loved every piece of The Crystal Heart, purely and passionately. How could something so pure, something that inspired life, light, and even pure love do such a terrible thing.

She didn't want to use Kinley's piece of the heart to kill him. She reached in her own back pocket and pulled out the parcel. She shed the leather outer coat from the shard slowly, taking in the feeling of the leather on her fingers. She ran her fingers over the shard that was resting on the leather, it was warm to the touch and it pulsated under her fingers. A pained look seemed to take over her face. She placed the point of it on Kinley's chest and closed her eyes.

Her hands were shaking, *Stop it Arissa, you need to be steady.* It was the Man-Gods voice again, this time she was awake, how was this possible. *You need to make sure that I touch his heart, plunge me in as far as you can.*

Arissa paused, and then replied through her own thoughts. *He is beautiful, what changed him?*

The Man-God replied *I did, he looks like himself, but he looks like me, we are the same person, Arissa. I gave up myself, not knowing what was to come. I was very young when I placed my heart on the mountain, just a little older then Kinley, barely an adult. It's something that I wanted and something that I knew had to be done. It's the same with Kinley, he is terrified right now, but he trusts me. He knows that I love him, more than I love any other and I told him everything would be okay. Arissa, you need to trust me, this is what's best, for Kinley and for every Varian, Arathian or other. Kinley has to follow his destiny, for the good of everyone in Arathia, but in order to do that, you have to wake my love.*

There were sounds coming from outside the cart, but Arissa was too involved in what she was doing to care. She sat motionless for a moment, thinking about what The Crystal Heart had told her. The Man-God loved Kinley, and Kinley loved him. She knew this; it's why she finally stopped pursuing him, he would never be happy with her, because he didn't love her the same way that he did The Crystal Heart. The Shard had started cutting through his clothes; she took a deep breath and raised her available hand, slamming it down hard on the shard. She felt it slide through his skin easily. Kinleys eyes flew open and she was shocked to see that their color had changed.

The cyan in his eyes seemed to glow with the same blue light of the glow-grubs and the brown in them was darker, almost black. He opened his mouth as if to scream, but a gurgling sound was all that came out. Blood flowed up from his throat, and he started coughing.

His blood sprayed all over her face, silent tears rolled down her cheeks mixing with his blood. She looked down to where the shard was in his chest. Blood was welling up from where her hands still pressed it in, his clothes, which were the traditional white of the sick, were stained blood red.

Kinley gasped for breath, his face contorted in pain he arched his back, pressing into Arissa's hands, then collapsed. Arissa watched his eyes. The blood seemed to flow from between his lips forever; Arissa leaned down, her tears still falling. She kissed his cheek, the life drained from his eyes as they went dull. She looked into them, no longer shining, no longer showing any spark of life. Kinley was dead, and she had killed him.

Shouting was coming from outside, Arissa was worried that someone had heard the commotion coming from inside the covered cart. She wiped off the last of her tears and some of the blood from her face. After double checking that his chest was no longer rising and falling with the breathe of life, she pulled the shard of The Crystal Heart out of Kinleys chest, she almost expected his body to move in protest, but it didn't happen. She looked at the shard in her hand, it looked as dead as Kinley did, opaque, metallic, simply empty.

It came out of his chest clean; Arissa wrapped it back up in leather, tied it off and placed in her back pocket. The blood on the floor of the cart was rapidly disappearing; it seeped into the wood, just like when Kinley had cut himself in the tent. The wood seemed thirsty for it and drank in every drop that touched it. The only blood left was that on Arissa's body and on Kinleys body. With a jolt the cart rocked back and forth, there were more sounds coming from outside the cart. The stench of death was in the air, was it possible that the rest of the tribe could smell it too, would they come running to the cart?

Arissa went to the door, casting one last look back at Kinley. She opened the flap of the tent and poked her head through, her face still spattered with blood. Arissa wasn't expecting the scene that lay before her eyes. The people of her tribe were running back and forth in chaos.

Arissa tried to focus her eyes on the direction where the people were running from, but the darkness wouldn't allow it. She jumped from the cart and landed in a somersault, twisting around to stand on her feet, she blew into a full run towards the back of the group, not even thinking about what Fallyn had told her about staying out of a battle while she was unprotected by armor.

The first thing that she was able to see was flaming arrows flying towards a group of glowing white creatures. *The Ree-Kyae, when did they catch up?* Arissa didn't even think about what she was doing. She barreled into the group, still angry and laden with pain at having to watch Kinley die. Arissa went ballistic taking one Ree-Kyae down after another, pulling at their heads, breaking their necks, knocking them down and driving the heel of her foot onto their skulls. She moved from one evil creature to the next, allowing her rage build with each. They were at fault, they broke the heart, and if it weren't for them then she wouldn't have had to kill Kinley.

She tore through a group of Ree-Kyae, ignoring blows to her head, bites on her arms and scratches on her face. There was one Ree-Kyae at the back of the group doing battle with Peadar. This one was bigger than the others were, it definitely looked like the leader of the group, and Arissa blamed everything on him. She cursed him with every word that she knew before running at him, screaming as if she was possessed. She launched herself from the ground, kicking the big Ree-Kyae in the chest, knocking it backwards, unfortunately, it was faster and more agile then she had given credit.

While the big Ree-Kyae was in midair, it somersaulted, twisting its body, not only landing on its feet but also facing her. It snarled, then in a whispery and strained voice it said, "Where is he, we know he is here."

There was only one person in the tribe that Arissa could think would bring any attention to it. *Kinley,* she thought, *it has to be talking about Kinley.*

"He is dead," Arissa said, "I suggest you call off your fighters and surrender, or you will soon join him."

"You lie." Was all that the Ree-Kyae said, Peadar looked at her then came closer.

"Arissa this is the leader of this group, if we

take him out the others will fall back, and I don't think it's going to give up."

"Then we have to kill him."

At that moment, the Ree-Kyae leapt from his stance, pointed teeth aiming straight for Arissa. She dodged its charge and came back around. The shard of The Crystal Heart in her back pocket had started heating up and then something occurred to her. If just the light of The Crystal Heart is enough to kill them, stabbing them with a piece of the actual heart should be more than enough.

Arissa jumped out of the way right as a glowing ball of gnashing teeth and sharp claws came at her, it moved past her as she sidestepped it.

"Peadar," She yelled, "Help!"

Peadar jumped on the Ree-Kyae's back, forcing it to the ground, Arissa took advantage, of this, and she pulled the shard out of her back pocket, quickly unwrapped it and, for the second time that day, drove it into a living creature's chest. This time however, the creature would not wake up.

Peadar grabbed the Ree-Kyae's head and twisted it as hard as he could, breaking its neck with a loud crack. Arissa looked towards the rest of the ground, surreptitiously wrapping the shard back up in the leather and sliding it into her back pocket. The other Ree-Kyae were falling back due to lack of direction, but not fast enough for her to call it a win. Arissa, once again, plunged headfirst into the battle that was still taking place. Viciously grabbing at whatever Ree-Kyae she could get her hands on, breaking whatever limb she was able to, trying to inhibit any form of attack on anyone else. She was still reeling with rage at what they had made her to do

Kinley, but now it was slightly under control, or at least better directed

Everything that she could see in the dark world was red. There was blood everywhere, and the bodies on the ground were almost indistinguishable from each other. *There is nothing like this.* She thought. She was right too, there was pure terror on almost every Varian face, the stench was horrible as it radiated off the Ree-Kyae's rotting flesh. The only smell that came close to overpowering it was the smell of blood, hot and salty. The Ree-Kyae saw that they were losing the battle; they started retreating, some of them limping and cradling their arms as they ran. The Varians with swords were already going around the battlefield making sure that what corpses were there, were actually dead. Flaming arrows still flew in the direction that the Ree-Kyae were running, the flames made it easier to see if they struck a Ree-Kyae in the darkness.

Arissa slipped away from the battlefield to her tent where she slipped into some clean clothes so she wouldn't be caught on the battlefield after Fallyn had told her not to be there. After she was all cleaned off, she made her way over to Esras' cart to check on Kinley. Arissa could smell fish cooking over the fires; it was going to be nice to have something in her stomach again. She took the familiar path through the carts to Esras' cart, which she was shocked to find unmanned. Arissa climbed up the front of the covered cart, and entered expecting there to be more people in there then she had ever seen. She was wrong.

Her face fell, not even Kinley was in there. She was suddenly stricken with fear; I hope they aren't putting him with the rest of the dead. She rushed out of the cart back to the battlefield. The first person that she came across was Peadar, who was in worse condition that she had left him after their battle at Kieron's cart. This battle had obviously taken its toll on the fighters as well as the other Varians in the tribe.

"Peadar, where's Kinley?" Arissa frantically exploded.

"I haven't seen him here? I imagine that he is in Esras' cart still. Is he dead? I thought he was just sick."

"I have no time to explain right now, he's not in the healer's cart." Arissa said, turning to walk away from Peadar.

"What happened to sharing a meal?" he asked her but she hadn't heard him. She just continued to walk around looking at the faces of the dead fighters. A lot of the woman had lost partners, some of the children had lost their fathers, and she had lost Kinley. She had lost her best friend. Tears started rolling down her cheeks. Arissa walked around aimlessly, and then went off looking for Enat.

She didn't know how she would break the news to her. How do you tell somebody's mother that because of a dream, you stabbed her only son, and then he was taken from his resting place to be buried with the dead from a battle that you left him to fight? Tears kept rolling down her cheeks as she looked through the crowds of people, Arissa had no clue if Enat had set up her own camp this time, or if she was still staying with Keeva. Tears were being shed in almost every direction that Arissa looked.

Mothers were with their children crying or calming them down, there were women who were in relationships this morning, and now found themselves single and crying, holding something that had belonged to their lost loves.

The Crystal Heart: Beginnings

This is what battle and war does to people, Arissa thought as she looked around for a high spot where the families had set up their tents. If not for the glowing fires, she wouldn't have been able to see anything. She surveyed the area, until she found the deep wine purple of Keeva's tent. She ran towards it, leaping over a few obstacles in her way, trying to keep Keeva's tent in her sight through the darkness. When she arrived at the tent, she stopped briefly to see if she could find anyone around, but Keeva and Enat were nowhere to be seen. She plunged directly into the tent.

*   *   *

Kinley was sitting at the lush green moss in the memories of The Crystal Heart. He had taken the shard out of his back pocket and removed it from the tied leather package. He had become accustomed to holding the warm pulsating object on his bear skin; the small amount of heat that it radiated comforted him.

He knew it was going to happen soon. His love had told him that, but he didn't know how soon. Another thing that Kinley wanted to know, very badly, was what part he played in the plan that his love had already put into motion. This was something that Kinley was planning to get to the bottom of before he was to wake up. He didn't want to be thrown back into his world, separated from his love, especially with no idea of what he was supposed to do.

"My love," he said, "why is it so difficult to measure time, both here and there. There is either constant light or no light at all."

The Crystal Heart replied, "I wanted to do that because I wanted all Varians safe from the Ree-Kyae.

If I allowed any form of darkness to fall, they would charge out during it, still hunting."

Kinley thought to himself for a moment, and then asked the question he was meaning to, "I know I have asked you this before, but what part am I to play in your plan?"

"I am surprised that you still don't see it, without you my plan wouldn't exist. Kinley I want to be put back together. I have told your mother this, but what I haven't told her is that only you can do it."

"Only me? Is it only me because of the love that we share? Is there another reason that I am the only one?" Kinley started hyperventilating; the pressure of the words had started sinking in.

"Love, calm down. You are the only one for a few reasons. You are the only person that I have known before they even knew themselves. I trust you. Anyone can gather the pieces and put them together, some already have started at my request, but you are the only one who could make me whole again."

"Why is that?" Kinley asked he was going to finish his question with why am I the only one who can make you whole?" but before he was able to get it out he felt a dull ache in his chest. He started gasping for air, and noticed that the pain in his chest was also coupled with a pulling.

Kinleys hand shot to his chest, he clenched his hand to a fist and pressed it to the pain.

"What's wrong my love?" The Crystal Heart asked him with a slight sense of urgency. "The pain." Was all that Kinley could manage, he screamed as loud as he could and pulled his fist back. It was covered in thick warm blood.

He looked to his chest. His clothing was

covered in red stickyness. His arms and legs started flailing, and he couldn't control them.

"It's okay my love, be calm." The Crystal Heart said, Kinley heard it, but just barely. He squeezed his eyes shut, hoping that this pain would all somehow disappear, but the pain stayed. When he opened them, he saw Arissa standing over him. His eyes were fixed on her face; there were crimson drops like rubies that clung to her moonlight skin. Tears slid down her cheeks. The pain in his chest was terrible; he had never felt anything like it before.

It was as if someone had left a sharp stone on the fire, and then while it was still red hot shoved it directly through his body, past his bone and directly into his heart. His vision started fading to black, he could feel Arissa's hand on his chest, pressing down on the shard. The very last thing Kinley was able to feel was a soft brush of lips against his cheek, and then he was dead.

The next thing he knew, he was being moved still unconscious, *What, what happened?* Kinley thought, unable to speak. He tried to remember what happened, he remembered sitting in the moss talking to his love, then there was a pain in his chest and he remembered.

I died! Now what do I do, how do I wake up? Kinley heard faint voices in the background.

"Lay him down, he needs to rest."

"Do you think we should splash some water on him Enat?" who did these voices belong to, the first one was his mothers, and the second, Kinley strained to remember through a thick fog, the second one was Keeva.

"No," Enat said, "no water, he'll be fine, we just have to wait." Kinley tried to understand what they were saying but he couldn't seem to grasp the meaning of any of the words.

She must have done it, he thought, *she must have been able to kill me. Why am I still not awake, did she miss the heart?* He knew that couldn't be the case, he knew that Arissa had hit the right spot because he felt it when the shard had pierced his chest.

My love, have you left me? Kinley thought.

No, I haven't left you, I have never left you, nor will I ever leave you.

What happened? I thought I was supposed to wake up after I was stabbed by the shard.

You will my love, you will. You just have to be patient; your body has to heal before it's able to perform even the most basic functions.

So am I fine? I can't move, I can't speak, and I can't even see what's going on around me, but I will be okay?

Yes love, you will be better then you were before, you just died love, you have to allow your body to recuperate.

I love you.

I love you, too.

With the last I love you, Kinley allowed The Crystal Heart to trail off. He tried to sleep, to make the time pass faster, but apparently, one cannot sleep in death, they can only listen. Kinley's eyes were open, Arissa had not closed them once he had died, but he couldn't see anything. Kinley knew things, but didn't know how he knew them. He knew that Enat had washed the blood from his body, but he couldn't feel anything. He knew when Keeva was there, and when she wasn't, though he couldn't see her.

He had no desire to eat, no need to, because he was dead. He knew when he was moved, though he couldn't feel anything on his skin. He just seemed anchored to his body, as if it was a casket around him as opposed to being a part of him.

As time passed, he felt more and more connected, but the only one of the five senses that he had was sound. Eventually he felt his heart start beating again, a while later he was able to start breathing again, it started by a fit of coughing up thick clots of blood, but still he lay there unable to control his own body. *It won't be much longer love, I promise you.* The Crystal Heart chimed in.

Very slowly his senses started returning to him, his sense of touch started at his fingertips, spreading down his fingers, and up his arms to his chest, reaching down to the very tips of his toes. His sense of smell restored, and he wished that it hadn't. The air around him reeked with the stench of death.

It's coming from me, was all that he thought. His mouth was extremely dry, and tasted so; he noticed how his tongue was sticking to the roof of his mouth.

"Keeva, get in here, I think he is going to wake up, bring some light so he can see us." Enat called from next to him.

Blurrily and from darkness, the surrounding area started coming into view.

"Look at his eyes." Keeva said and a gasp from Enat followed. "They looked foggy when we brought him in, didn't they? They look like they just keep getting brighter, he must be coming back." Kinley started getting excited; he was only moments away from getting to see his mother again, after so long. Kinley tried to blink his eyes, and was successful, the moisture on them felt good. It helped his vision as well; he blinked a few more times until he could see the people standing over him.

Arissa wasn't present, and even though it didn't surprise him, he was slightly disappointed. Keeva looked the same, the same moonlight skin, the same dark brown eyes, the same shoulder cropped black hair shining in the light of the glow-grubs she held in her hand.

Kinley was very surprised when he saw his mother. Something had changed about her, but it wasn't exactly in her physical appearance. It was in her demeanor, she was stronger, more self-reliant, more sure of herself.

Kinley closed his eyes and opened them back up, checking to see if his mother would look the same or if she was going to continue being the new cold person that was looking down on him. Her eyes bore into him with deep intensity, she was waiting for him to say something, to acknowledge that they were looking at him. It finally occurred to him that what she was looking for was a true sign of life. He opened and closed his mouth a few times to moisten his tongue and mouth; he noticed Enat and Keeva holding their breaths.

"Ma?" his voice sounded scratchy and unused, also deeper. Keeva had burst out into tears at the sound of his voice.

"Kinley?" His mother said, her words sounding firm and strong, this was definitely not something he was used to.

"Kinley, I've missed you so much, can you move?"

"I don't know Ma, I haven't tried, I am alive right, I'm not dreaming?"

"No, you aren't dreaming, baby, you are alive."

Everything felt so different here than the

dream world. He had forgotten what the actual air felt like when it blew. He had forgotten the touch of his mother's skin on his until now. Her hand gently ran across his face in a gesture that he was familiar with, but also a gesture that didn't suit this new version of his mother.

Kinley had never had to put so much effort into moving his own body before. He concentrated hard on just lifting a finger and when he felt that finger move, he got excited and decided to try lifting his arm, though it felt more weighted down then his finger.

His eyes squinted and the sweat started beading on his forehead, slowly his arm began to rise. As it lifted Kinley could hear footsteps outside, he let it drop back down just as the tent flap flung open and Arissa barreled inside.

"Enat, I'm sorry, I don't know where he went…" She began but then caught sight of Kinley lying on the dirt floor of the tent. "I didn't want to do it, I didn't want to kill him." she said dropping to her knees beside him, tears already formed in her eyes released. "He said that he would come back Enat, I promise, he said that he would come back." she rested her hand over his heart as Enat laid her hand on Arissa's shoulder.

"I know Arissa, and he has. He is back." Enat looked down at Kinley; Keeva sat next to her, nodding.

"Yes, I am alive, Arissa you did very well." Kinley spoke. Arissa's mouth dropped and the tears that were on her cheek now flowed vigorously over her lips.

"I was just trying to move when you came in; if I knew it was you I wouldn't have dropped my arm."

"Oh Kinley," She said wrapping her arms around him as he lay there, "you have no idea how much I have missed you. I was so worried that I had dreamt the whole thing and that you weren't going to come back."

"I think I am starting to get the picture." Kinley said with a chuckle to himself. "If you don't mind though, I would like to stretch my muscles a little bit."

"Uh, sure," she said, releasing her hold on him and wiping her eyes, "go ahead." Arissa sat straight up and watched intently.

Everyone in the room sitting around Kinley had leaned forward to watch him try to move his limbs once more. Slowly his arm began to rise from the ground; even Kinley had managed to turn his head to see it. Once it rose, Kinley gently lowered it back to the ground, then moved the other one up, and lowered that one. He slid his palms up bending his elbows out, then pushing on the ground to raise his body. Pain shot through him, he hadn't used these muscles in a long time, and though they got bigger, they seemed weak from lack of use.

Kinley started noticing the changes that had taken place. His skin was darker, tan, but even more then his mothers. From what he could see of his arms, his muscle definition was much more pronounced then it had been.

"Can I please see myself?" Kinley asked to no one particular.

"There's something that you need to know, hun." Enat started.

"My love told me that I would look different, I just want to see how different I look." Enat looked at him, surprised. At first Kinley thought that her surprise was in the fact that had interrupted her, but her next question clarified.

"Your love?" Enat asked.

"Yes Ma, my love. I am in love with someone very special; you knew this the whole time though. Ma, I am in love with the Man-God, or more specifically, his heart."

This really surprised Enat, she did know that he was meant for someone outside the tribe, but she didn't imagine that it was the Man-God. The dreams made sense to her now. Someone was going to have to put it together, all the information about Kinley that she had been getting from The Crystal Heart. Her mouth dropped open.

"It's... It's you, isn't it? You're the one?" Keeva and Arissa looked at Enat, obviously unaware of what she was getting at. Kinley's eyes locked on his mothers. For quite a while, nothing was being said between anyone.

"Do you know more about this then I do?" Kinley's voice was serious; Enat finally broke the stare that had been going on between them by glancing at the ground. "Ma, do you know more about the plans that my love has for me then I do?" Enat looked back to Kinley then spoke.

"Keeva, Arissa, may I ask the two of you to leave, please? Kinley and I need to talk." Arissa and Keeva slowly moved out the tent flap, not wanting to leave.

"Kinley, come here, close to me, there are details about my past that you need to know. I have kept you sheltered as long as I could, but now things must come to light, starting with your conception."

Kinley moved closer to his mother, the strength returning to his limbs. He waited patiently for his mother to begin.

"I never wanted to tell you this because I never wanted you to feel like I loved you less because of it. Kinley your father was not a good man. He was attractive, that was true, but he was bullheaded and a pig. You're father always got what he wanted, except for one thing, me. You're father wanted me to the point where it drove him mad. This was during the time of The Crystal Heart, one of the last times that it stood whole on the mountain. I was not always the weak broken woman that raised you."

"I used to be strong, defiant and stubborn, if I was weak then you're father would have gotten away with what he did, but he broke me. We were stopped; we traveled a lot less back then because there was no fear from the Ree-Kyae. I was exhausted; I had just gotten back from a swim with Keeva, and made my way to my tent. I started to put on some dry clothes and heard the tent flap flutter, I figured that it was just the wind, but it wasn't. Hands grabbed around my waist and spun me around, and I was dazed. He pressed his lips to mine, probing with his tongue. I bit down as hard as I could on it, and he got angry with me. He pushed me backwards and I fell, hitting my head, then he took what he wanted from me, without my permission. I was so… violated."

"I reported him to the council and they handed down the punishment for rape. Torture, castration and banishment. The middle one I did myself. The tribe then packed up and moved on but not me. I followed him, I watched your father be abducted by the Ree-Kyae, and I laughed when it happened. I observed the

Ree-Kyae's movement for a while, keeping an eye out for anything different. It was during this period that I learned I was pregnant with you. There had been a lot of Ree-Kyae activity surrounding The Crystal Heart so I made my way up the mountain."

"It was littered with all types of garbage, bones from who knows what types of animals, sticks, stones, the Ree-Kyae would throw things at The Crystal Heart, trying to shatter it. I reached The Crystal Heart in time to see your father climbing out of a hole directly underneath. I watched him walk closer to it and try to move it with his hands. When he picked up a long bone and began to swing it, I cried out for him to stop and that he had a child, but I was too late, The Crystal Heart shattered. One of the pieces ricocheted off of the rock behind it and lodged into his skull, killing him instantly."

"A second piece of it came directly at me; it stuck into my arm, and instantly healed. I now understand that this piece of The Crystal Heart affected you, while you were inside me." Enat paused for a moment, catching her breath; Kinley said nothing, but still sat, waiting patiently for his mother to continue the story.

"I have been having dreams for a while now, with a voice. The voice had never confirmed who I thought it was. It told me where to find you after you had been bitten by that fish. It told me that Arissa was going to kill you. It told me that you would be all right, but Kinley, that voice also told me that someone was going to piece The Crystal Heart back together. What I didn't know was that someone was you. I don't know if it's you because of the shard that still lays in my arm, or the fact that both your parents were there when The

Crystal Heart was shattered, or the fact that your father was the one who shattered it."

Kinley was speechless; he had never thought that his mother carried such a secret. "Who knows?" was the first thing that Kinley thought to ask.

"Most people know the main details, about your father, and a little bit about what involved me, it's in the story of the shattering of The Crystal Heart. Keeva knows that I was up there watching your father, but not about the shard in my arm, and she knows that The Crystal Heart has been giving me dreams." Kinley's shock was starting to wear off, now a little bit of anger, disappointment and resentment was settling in.

"Ma, why would you tell Keeva and not me?" Enat looked Kinley directly in the eyes, for the first time since he had been brought back to life, she looked the same as before he died. Broken down and hurt, Enat's eyes drifted to the floor.

"I told you honey, I didn't want you to think that I loved you less."

"Ma, that wasn't your fault. There is no way that it would have made me think that you loved me any less."

"Good," She said helping Kinley stand, "now let's go get something to eat." Enat opened the tent flap and rotten smelling air flooded through the gap.

"What is that smell, what happened?" Kinley found himself choking out the words.

"The Ree-Kyae attacked while you were… incapacitated." Enat explained.

"I can't believe how dark it is. I never really noticed until I spent so much time in the light." Kinley walked next to his mother until they joined Keeva and

Arissa by the fire. He noticed that the lack of light left him slightly disorientated; he found himself leaning on Enat watching her feet and using them as a guide for where to step. Arissa and Keeva greeted them with a hug, first for Kinley then Enat.

"I've missed you so much." Arissa said in Kinley's ear during their hug.

I know, Kinley thought to himself, *but now it's time for things to change.*

Kinley noticed movement off to the side of Keeva's tent, and looked towards it. He was surprised when Peadar walked out from behind it; and even more surprised when Arissa's face lit up.

Maybe they already have.

"I'm sorry," Peadar said, "Kinley! I didn't know you were doing better, but I guess with the attack and all…" his voice trailed off.

"I'll be right there, just give me a moment." Arissa said, watching him with intense eyes. She looked strange to Kinley, she reminded him of the brown furry creatures in The Crystal Hearts memories.

"Go," he said to her, "and have fun." Kinley winked at her and a wink was returned. Arissa walked over to Peadar, she looked to the ground, then back up at him. Peadar walked out of Kinley's view, Arissa turned towards him. He smiled at her again and waved as she turned back and followed Peadar to his camp.

"Looks like Arissa found someone to keep her… occupied while I was out." Enat nodded in agreement., a smile on her face and eyes on him "A lot of things have changed. Arissa is now walking with the men. She was fighting alongside them when the Ree-Kyae attacked. We have been divided, some people feel that she shouldn't be fighting; others see her as a strong beacon of hope. I expect things will be getting a lot worse now that so many have lost lovers and children." Keeva told Kinley, giving him a brief update on all that had happened.

The look on Enats face wasn't affected by what she had said. Enat sat by the fire, motioning for Kinley to join her. Kinley could smell the fish cooking. He arched his back, stretching his arms to the sky and yawned before walking over to her. He noticed that the ground was cold, something that he hadn't felt since before he was in the warm and lit world of The Crystal Hearts memories. He was filled with a longing for the warm bright world, and the company of The Crystal Heart.

My love? He thought, and then waited for a response, but nothing came. He looked from the fish lying on the coals of the fire, to his mother and Keeva, then in the direction that Arissa walked away. He was surrounded by everyone that he loved but Kinley felt alone. Keeva took the fish off the fire; the fillet flaked to pieces as she divided it up between the three. She handed some to Enat and Kinley and three of them ate mostly in in silence accompanied by the dim light of the fire.

Over the meal a few pleasant words were said but nothing important, Keeva had already said all that he wanted to know. Kinleys mind wrestled with that, as well as what his mother told him and all of this without the voice of The Crystal Heart to help him sort it out correctly.

Across the temporary camping area, Arissa was sitting on a stone that had been chiseled into the shape of a chair. A fire was roaring in front of her and Peadar sat next to her, she noticed that his leg nervously jumped up and down in rhythm. Caedmon was on the other side of the fire, poking at it with a long, pointed, rod. Arissa wasn't sure if it was a dried up branch off one of the skeletal remainders of the trees.

Something gave her the feeling it was actually a long chipped away stone, but for a stranger reason she felt that it was inappropriate to ask. Caedmon always had this strange staff with him, due to his limp, and Arissa couldn't remember ever seeing him without it. Peadar attempted to make conversation while his grandfather was cooking, but Arissa was preoccupied with the day's events. She had been looking down while he spoke, her head snapped up.

Interrupting him, she asked "Peadar, what weapon do you think Kieron is going to make for me? After this stop, I should be outfitted with my armor and equipped with my weapon. I have never used one before though. I don't even know how to hold a sword." He looked at her, trying to decide what he should say.

"I honestly have no clue Arissa, you are a unique case, and a woman has never been a fighter. I have seen you in action though, more than most people have, and honestly I don't think that you need a weapon."

Arissa bit her lip, and moved her eyes to the ground. She was learning how to manipulate quickly and she wanted something. "Do you think that...I could maybe... try your sword?" she asked slowly, a mock sense of insecurity in her voice. Peadar looked at her, unsure of what to do.

A smile crossed his face, "I've underestimated you before, and I don't think it would be a wise move to do it again." Caedmon watched sneakily through the flame, Arissa thought that she saw a the flame temporarily part, but couldn't be sure. "So, would that be a yes?"

She looked at him and a slightly embarrassed smile crept over her face. Peadar looked at her, and reached toward the hilt of his sword. A smile crossed his face this time, and he pulled his hand away quickly.

"One thing you have to understand about your weapon, Arissa, is that your weapon becomes part of yourself. My sword, for instance, is an extension of my arm. They are very precious because of what they are made of as well. The materials that are used are either difficult to make or extremely rare, so most people only get one weapon. When you get yours from Kieron you will have to go through the same ceremony that we all did, then you will understand why I can't let you even hold mine."

Arissa's smile faded to a frown, but she accepted is response, she felt slightly foolish for even asking.

"Hey, it's okay, don't upset yourself over nothing. Trust me with this, Kieron will make you a beautiful weapon, though it will pale to your brilliance. It will be one of a kind, and if it's even half as deadly as you are, then you'll understand."

Arissa shook her head, she still felt foolish so she redirected their conversation to something a little more common, "How's the fish coming along Caedmon?"

Caedmon had a jar in his hand; he was sprinkling something onto the fish. Arissa hadn't seen this before, normally the fish just is thrown onto a hot and very flat rock sitting in the coals of the fire, but

Caedmon seemed to be caring for it.

"Fish can be very... plain, tonight is something special, I guarantee it." He spoke cryptically, not wanting to give his secrets away. He hobbled over to her, staff in hand, "Stick out your tongue." He commanded, and without hesitation, Arissa obeyed. "Close your eyes." Again, a command and again she obeyed.

Something small and light hit her tongue, her face changed instantly; she brought her tongue back into her mouth and scraped it against the roof of her mouth a couple of times trying to get the new taste off of it. Both Peadar and Caedmon started laughing at her reaction. "What is that stuff?" she asked when she was finally satisfied with the lack of the new taste in her mouth. "I feel like I have tasted it before, but I can't figure out where."

"You have been in the water, haven't you, at one point or another? This water has been passed through many layers of cloth and leathers, then boiled down to these little white flakes. I sprinkle a little of them on the fish and it takes on a completely new taste. Just can't put too much on there, found that out the hard way, didn't we Peadar?" He nodded in reply to the old man who let out another loud laugh then went back to his tending of the fish. "It's almost done by the way." Caedmon called out over the fire.

As Caedmon poked around at the fish with his staff and kept sprinkling the little white crystals on it, Arissa chose to get to know Peadar a little better.

"What happened to your parents, I mean, you live with your grandfather, where are they?" She asked him. Peadar looked down uncomfortably; Arissa got the feeling that, for the second time that night, she had asked the wrong thing. They both sat in silence; Peadar seemed to be staring off into space.

"Don't keep the she-fighter waiting, Peadar. If you do that you may end up on the ground again." A chuckle came from behind the fire where Caedmon was preparing the fish. Arissa was glad to see another side to the old man, but now the look on Peadars face worried her.

"You don't have to answer, so you know."

"No, it's okay, you aren't the first person to ask, and I am sure you won't be the last, so I just need to get over it."

"Okay…?" Arissa answered.

"Why do you fight the Ree-Kyae?" His question caught her off guard.

"I fight for my friends and my family." She said failing to see his point.

"Good, so do I." he said, "The Ree-Kyae are the reason that I live with Gramps. My parents are dead. The Ree-Kyae killed them."

Chapter Five

Armor and Weapon

Arissa enjoyed her time with Peadar, and everything progressed smoothly. Peadar told Arissa of his different battles, she wasn't even aware that their tribe had so many fights. He told her of battles with the Ree-Kyae, and even other tribes that travel the five rivers to the Varian Trading Post. Arissa was amazed that, even though all Varians had a common enemy, they still fought against each other.

The fish that Caedmon had made was delicious, the best that Arissa had ever tasted. It wasn't plain, the flavors in it seemed to have been nurtured into fruition, she put the first bite in her mouth expecting it to taste just like the white flakes that Caedmon had put on her tongue, instead it seemed that the flakes complimented the natural taste of the fish and brought out even more subtle flavors.

Still though, in the back of her mind, Arissa couldn't help but wonder what the plan that The Crystal Heart had for Kinley was. She tried to put it out of her head and concentrate on Peadar and Caedmon and their stories but no matter how hard she tried, the question was always there, gnawing at her. When the meal was finished they sat and talked, Caedmon told stories of when The Crystal Heart was up, and light was brightly illuminating each corner of Arathia and even further. Arissa couldn't seem to get into them, normally she loved hearing stories of the world where The Crystal Heart hung high, now she felt she didn't need the stories because she had seen it with her own eyes.

Arissa yawned, feigning tiredness, "Sorry Peadar, I have a lot of things I have to do when I wake up, and getting my armor is one of them. I still want to check up on Kinley before I go to sleep too, you came to get me right when he… woke up, and so I haven't had a chance to talk to him yet."

"That's fine," he said, "but I get to walk you back to Keeva's tent." He said, reasoning with her.

They walked side by side looking at the ground, "What are you thinking about?" Arissa asked him, she could tell that there was something on his mind.

"I am trying to decide." was all that he said.

"On…?" Arissa pressed leaving it open-ended. Arissa stopped for a moment and looked around; Keeva's tent was already in sight and was getting closer to them with each step.

"Well…" He stalled, trying to make it where he didn't have to answer. She estimated the distance between them and the tent; they were going to be there in just a few steps.

"Oh just spit it out before you don't have a chance to anymore."

Still stopped Peadar turned around he looked nervous as he spoke, "Well... on this."

He leaned in and kissed her on the mouth. Arissa returned his kiss, and found her hands grabbing at his hair pulling his face in closer to hers.

"Sorry," he said when they had parted, "I've wanted to do that all night, and I decided that you would appreciate it if gramps left it out of his story. I mean, it is about you and I would hate to steal the spotlight with my rugged good looks."

Arissa looked up at him; a cocky grin was spread wide across his face. "...and you had to ruin it." she said sarcastically, stretching out the word had and saying the whole sentence in a singsong rhythm.

She playfully gave Peadar an open palmed slap on the shoulder as he turned to walk away. As he was turning she pulled him close to her, gave him a kiss on his cheek, turned, and walked to Kinley. Peadar stood there for a moment, dumbfounded, then walked back to his camp.

Arissa had a huge smile as she walked over to Kinley, Enat and Keeva. The four of them talked for a while, they stayed away from conversation relating to the Ree-Kyae attack or the ordeal that Kinley had gone through. Eventually they paired off and Keeva and Enat started their own conversation, while Arissa and Kinley spoke to each other. He wanted to bring up the shards and what The Crystal Heart had said his part in everything would be; but there would be much more time to figure that out.

Sitting around the fire with Arissa brought back a sense of normalcy and he was planning on bathing in that for a while before bringing up anything else that would plunge him back into the different world he was now part of. They sat, talking until they couldn't keep their eyes open any longer. Almost everyone around them was already asleep. Keeva only had the two beds in the tent, one for her and one for Enat, so Kinley slept on the dirt floor.

Lying there, he started thinking about his life since he found the shard. It seemed like forever ago to him, most of it spent while he was in the memories of The Crystal Heart. His head started to hurt so he closed his eyes, and he drifted peacefully to sleep, the radiating pain in his head faded into the bright white light of The Crystal Heart.

*   *   *

Kinley was kneeling by a river. He knew this one was one of the five rivers that connected at the Trading Post, but he wasn't sure which. The whole world was bright; he seemed to be back in the memories of The Crystal Heart only this time he couldn't pick his own course. He looked down into the water, and could see the bottom, but something was different. There were no plants and a sandy bottom, instead of the rocky bottom he saw while he was in the memories of his love. Another difference was that he didn't see the little fish from before. Instead, staring up at him from the depths of the river was the acid green fish that put him into his coma. The four whiskers on each side of its face twitched as water moved through its mouth and gills. Kinley looked down at it and cocked his head wondering why it was just sitting there, watching him.

He was surprised that he didn't feel anger towards this creature, instead he felt as if he were visiting his old friend. It rose from the bottom bringing its nose to the surface of the water, its dorsal fin broke the surface sending a wave of ripples across, and a small splashing sound could be heard. Kinley was calm. The fish sunk back down and before his eyes could adjust to follow it down, he caught a glimpse of his reflection in the water. He concentrated for a while on his reflection, noticing the differences between this new person looking back at him and the way he used to look. He reached his hand towards the barrier between wet and dry, he almost stuck his hand in, he would have if he didn't remember that the green fish was watching him from the bottom. He let his eyes focus back to the bottom of the river. The green fish was nowhere in sight.

He stuck his hand in the water, only it wasn't the normal cold, wetness of water, which he normally felt. Instead, he felt skin, his skin. He pressed in, noticing how the rippling of the water didn't affect the reflection. He touched the cheek of the reflection and could faintly feel his own fingers on his face. He moved his hand across his lips and up to his eye. A lot had changed.

When he was able to tear his eyes away from the reflection, he noticed that someone was kneeling next to him in the reflection. His head turned, expecting to see someone, but no one was there. He looked down at the water and the person was still there.

"Is that you?" Kinley asked aloud. His voice

seemed to be made of two different voices.

The one he had known forever and one with a gurgling undertone. He watched the person kneeling next to him. The most dominate feature on his face were his eyes. They were a bright blue, and seemed to shine and generate their own light; their color matched the new blue in Kinley's own eyes. The other reflection had dark curly hair, it was right on the line between brown and black, the hair swayed with the motion of the river and hung half way down the forehead. His face was perfectly sculpted, the most beautiful person that Kinley had ever seen. His lips moved and Kinley heard a voice like the one that spoke to him in the memories of The Crystal Heart.

"Yes, it's me." It was as clear as the water Kinley was staring into, no gurgling or bubbling came through.

"You… you are amazing." Kinley stuttered in awe, with no control over the words that came out of his mouth. He also noticed that the gurgling undertone was no longer attached to his own voice. He looked straight into the water; his reflection no longer blocked his view.

"I want to do something." Kinley reached one hand toward the water as he spoke.

He leaned towards the water as his hand broke the surface. His head followed going under the water, he kept his eyes open, watching the kneeling figure before him. Bubbles rose from his nostrils and tickled the side of his face as they floated to the surface of the water. He felt his hair brushing the sides of his face as; it too, now swayed with the current of the river.

Kinley didn't stop moving forward until he felt his lips meet the lips of this reflection. Kinley closed his eyes; his lips prickled and tingled as they touched the ones in the water. He felt the water moving past his face with the current as well as the bubbles that were still rising from his clothing and hair from the air that he had brought down with him.

The white radiating light of The Crystal Heart was fading in behind his eyelids, getting brighter with each of the rhythmic beats. Kinley kept his eyes closed and pulled his head out of the water, still touching the face under it with his hand. "I love you." He said as he opened his eyes. Nothing was there, white light surrounded him, he couldn't feel the springy moss under his knee, there was no water dripping down his face, his hair was dry. The only sensation that he felt was the lingering prickle on his lips from the kiss that he and his love had shared. The last thing that he heard was the voice of The Crystal Heart.

"Even when you think I am not with you, I am. I will never leave you." Kinley didn't wake up instantly; instead, he kneeled there, in the same position surrounded by white waiting for his body to open its eyes, enjoying the sensation that was still dancing across his lips.

*   *   *

Kinley's eyes opened, both Enat and Keeva were still soundly asleep. Kinley looked around, wondering if he should attempt leaving, he knew one thing though; he wanted to tell Arissa about his dream. Kinley lay silent, going back and forth on getting up and going to find Arissa, and possibly waking Keeva or his mother in the process, or waiting until they woke up themselves. Finally, he decided on easing onto his knees and moving to the flap of the tent. When he was outside the tent, he stretched his arms to the permanently dark sky, arched his back, and yawned.

He had no idea how long he had been asleep; it was still quiet outside and very few people were up and moving around. Those that were watched him with a look of unfamiliarity on their faces.

Have I changed that much? Kinley thought as he walked past the gawking people and their tents. He easily found his way to Arissa's family tent, the green of the tent stood out around so many different shades of brown. Smoke still drifted up from the smoldering coals of the fire, Kinley sat by it, keeping warm and waiting for Arissa to wake up.

Time passed as he sat there, thinking about the things that had happened and trying to cope with what he just found out. He was going to be the one to search out and piece The Crystal Heart back together. He was the only one that could. *This is definitely a critical point in the Varian timeline.* Kinley thought. The Crystal Heart hasn't been gone for an extremely long time, only since his just before his birth, but that much time of nothing but darkness would be enough to leave a scar on any society.

He heard a stirring coming from inside the tent and waited, hoping that Arissa had woken up. Nobody came out of the tent, so Kinley sat back down allowing his mind to wander a little further. Kinley chewed on his lip, thinking about the dream he had. He remembered the tingling on his lips, the touch of his love's face against the palm of his hand. He wasn't sure that it was even real, he had been in and a part of many "real" dreams before, but in those he always had self-determination. In this one, he was no choice in what he could or couldn't do.

Kinley wondered if maybe it meant that he was in someone else's dream, a conscious body just going with the flow. His eyes closed as he leaned back, almost falling backwards. A deep breath was inhaled through his nostrils and blown out of his mouth as he thought. Kinley wanted The Crystal Heart with him again. Not even two sleeps ago, Kinley had been there, and they had been together. Another stirring came from inside the tent. Kinley got up from where he was sitting and strode over to it, peaking inside. Nothing moved but the sound was still coming. It was like a scratching sound. Kinley looked around but nothing seemed out of place, nothing except the fact that Arissa's family tent was empty, that is.

*   *   *

Arissa woke up to a shiver running down her spine; it seemed colder out than normal. She heard rustling outside her tent, and sprung up fiercely, not bothering to rub the sleep from her eyes. The first thought that popped into her head was that The Ree-Kyae were back. She leapt from the place she had been sleeping and tumbled out of the tent, stopping herself in an attack-ready pose.

Both feet were planted firmly on the ground, she had an animalistic snarl plastered across her face and her head was snapping back and forth at every sound as she tried to make her eyes penetrate the darkness around her. She was surprised to see that the only threat there possibly could have been was Peadar standing nervously by the glowing embers of what used to be the fire. He looked at her as if she was something to be feared. She softened her features and stance, and walked over to him.

"Hi Peadar," she said, "I didn't mean to scare you. What can I do for you?"

"Scare me?" he asked trying to put up a front. He puffed out his chest in an attempt to make himself look bigger then he was, which wasn't necessary. "You didn't scare me; I came because I had a message for you, from the armor maker."

Arissa watched him, a quizzical look on her face. She allowed the puzzlement to dissolve, and then each muscle in her face flexed giving the look that her expression was carved in stone. She nodded at Peadar and turned. He didn't bother following her; instead, he turned and went his own way. She made her way past the tents to the caravans.

I wonder why she sent Peadar instead of coming for me herself. Arissa looked ahead and could see one fire that was illuminating the caravans around it. Sitting directly in front of her was the armor maker's cart.

It stood a little taller than the other carts, and was covered with a bright orange canvas covering. There was what looked like a tube coming from of the top of the cart, almost at the center and smoke was rising from it. A sweet and smoky smell wafted through the air towards Arissa, The armor maker was burning incense. Arissa was confused again, incense was reserved for very special occasions, the floral and fruity parts of it were impossible to find since The Crystal Heart was shattered and nothing grew anymore. Arissa receiving her armor couldn't be important enough to burn incense.

Arissa grabbed the pole that protruded from the cart and swung up into the covered area. It was even smokier inside then out. The cart was dimly lit with small strange twinkling glow-grub bottles that had been strung from the top of the cart. She could just barely see the movement of the smoke in the dim light, sitting across from her was the armor maker, and a bundle was sitting on her lap. Her eyes and mouth were closed; she seemed content to be sitting there, enjoying the scent as she breathed in and out through her nose. *I wonder if she knows that I am here.* Arissa thought to herself as she cleared her throat, allowing the noise in order to announce her presence.

The woman sitting in front of her ignored the sound that she had made, Arissa decided that the appropriate thing to do now was to sit and wait. Arissa followed the example of the armor maker and closed her eyes and mouth, inhaling and exhaling the sweet smoke through her nose. She sat there for a while; appreciating the scent until she finally heard a noise, a clinking of metal and rustling of leather. She had sent the command to her brain to open her eyes, right before they opened; she saw fire behind her eyelids, fire and a deep red jewel. Then her eyes opened and the fire was gone. She blinked a few times, trying to bring it back, but it wouldn't return.

Arissa looked to where the armor maker was sitting when she closed her eyes; she now saw an empty space. She turned her head to try to locate the woman. She found the bundle sitting on a makeshift shelf jutting up from the floor at the far end of the cart. She walked over to it and picked it up, Arissa was surprised at how much it weighed, for such a small package it was extremely heavy. She noticed that there were two other packages of exactly the same size and shape sitting next to it, she hadn't even noticed them until she had picked up the one in her hands. The scratchy voice of the armor maker sounded from behind Arissa.

"Why did you pick that one up?" she asked.

"Excuse me?" Arissa asked, not knowing how to respond to the question.

"The one in your hands, why did you pick that one up as opposed to either of the other two on the table?" she repeated, adding a little more detail to her original question.

"I understood the question," stated Arissa, "I was just curious as to why it was important." The armor maker with the scratchy voice repeated her question, adding no more detail then she had before. Arissa gave up on getting any more information out of her and decided that it would be easier if she just answer the woman's question. "It was the only one I saw at the time." She said simply, looking into the armor makers eyes. Arissa let her head drop and she shrugged, the straight black hair rose and fell lightly with her shoulders as she did.

"You picked the right one." The armor maker said as she grabbed the bundle from Arissa. She unwrapped it and held up something very different then what Arissa had seen when she came in for her fitting. The armor that the armor maker held out to Arissa was beautiful. The metal was bright silver, so bright that it seemed to radiate a glow of its own. There were different pieces to the armor, what the armor maker was holding up now was the breastplate. Arissa held her hand out towards it and the armor maker handed the breastplate to her. On the front there was the metal, embossed on the metal was a very detailed design of a bird.

Arissa looked at the woman and asked, "What bird is this? It's beautiful."

"Fire-Bird." was all that the woman said. Arissa was unaware of any Fire-Bird in legend or lore. She couldn't bring anything up in her memory for the life of her. The bird had a straight beak, three feathers on the top of its head that curled back and then forward to a point. They were in a straight line and had what seemed like a round part right before the tip of the feather. They grew smaller as they went back, so the one in the front was the longest. The third one, on the very back of the bird's delicate looking head was the shortest.

The Fire-Bird seemed to be exploding upwards out of a blazing inferno. The flames from the inferno stretched to the very edge of the metal. The wings of the bird were outstretched starting in feathers but tapering off to flames at the back of the wing. Where the bird's eye was, a red jewel seemed to be stuck into the metal itself. Flames rose delicately from the Fire-Birds beak, flowing up over the breasts of the armor towards Arissa's face. The tail feathers were the last thing that Arissa noticed about the bird, though not for lack of detail, quite the opposite actually. They were extremely long and intricate, there were three of them and they seemed to wrap in and out of the flames, as if playing a game.

They flowed along the bottom of the breastplate and ended in the same sort of circle design that feathers on the head ended in, the circle right before the tip of the feather so it came to the same strange bulbous point. The back plate was connected to the breastplate with two leather straps that hung over the shoulders. Arissa flipped it around and saw the exact same image as on the front, but the scene was shown from the back. Both the breastplate and back plate were padded; Arissa guessed that there was sawdust packed between the leather and the metal it keep it soft. There were three leather straps on the sides, both on the breastplate and the back plate, to cinch the two together. She hadn't noticed but her jaw had fallen, showing how much she was amazed by the detail work on this one piece. She looked at the armor maker, who had a huge smile on her face now.

"What is the Fire-Bird?" Arissa asked again, still she got no answer from her. Instead, the armor maker held out two other pieces of armor.

They were the same piece of armor, but one was shaped differently than the other. One of them, the right one, covered only the upper arm and the shoulder, the metal used with these were embossed everywhere with raised flames, one after another, all the way up her arm. It left the forearm exposed. The one on the left arm went from shoulder to wrist; again, the flames seemed to flow up her arm to her shoulder. Where the elbow met there was leather to allow for flexibility, again at the shoulders. There were three leather straps on the right shoulder plate and five on the left, again, to tie it to her arm. Both were padded with the same sawdust as the breast and back plates. "May I put them on now?" Arissa asked.

The armor maker nodded her head, giving Arissa her Permission. Arissa handed the breast and back plates back to the armor maker, and then kneeled down to make it easier for the woman to fit them over her head. The armor maker then tied each of the three straps at her side. It fit Arissa perfectly. Arissa held out each arm and the woman secured the shoulder plates to her arms, tying them on the under-inside part of her arms. The woman looked at Arissa and handed her the next pieces, the leg shields.

These were split into two pieces, much like the shoulder plates. There was a part that protected the shins and a part that protected the thigh, both were metal, they were connected with leather, again for flexibility. Both of the metal pieces were decorated with the same heavily detailed embossed flames. The leg shields were padded the same as the other pieces. The right was different then the left as well with the leg shields. On the right leg shield there was a metal pocket on the outer side, embossed on that was another image of the Fire-Bird. On the leg the Fire-Bird, seemed to be stained orange and red, there was another red jewel where its eye was.

The armor maker allowed Arissa to take in the detail on the pouch and the detail on the rest of the metal then fastened them to her. They tied at the inner part of the leg, leaving very little vulnerable to attack. "What's this for?" Arissa asked holding her hand to the Fire-Bird embossed pocket on her outer right thigh. The woman held nothing else in her hands; she spoke one word "Weapon." Then she turned around and picked something up from the shelf behind her. She turned back towards Arissa, holding a helmet in her hand. This helmet looked like the head of the Fire-Bird that was embossed on her breastplate.

The straight beak seemed to jut out and down a little, there were larger red jewel eyes above the beak. The detail in the feathers on the helmet was like nothing else on the armor. Each feather seemed to stick out, the details in them perfect. The plume of feathers on the top of the head were just as she had seen on the breastplate, they curved back and then out towards the front with the same bulbous point at the tips. Arissa bent her head forward to accept the helmet. She closed her eyes as the armor maker placed it on her head. The helmet fit snugly, but Arissa was perfectly comfortable, the helmet was padded perfectly to fit her face. She turned her head back and forth, amazed at how heavy she now felt. She caught her head falling forward because of the weight of the helmet.

"Thank you, so much." She told the armor maker, "This is the most beautiful set of armor that I have ever seen."

"Let's hope that it functions as well as it looks," the armor maker told her, taking in the sight of Arissa's now armor clad body, "Kieron should be pleased that it matches his work. You're definitely something different Arissa, beautiful and deadly, just like the Fire-Bird."

With that, the armor maker turned away from her and held open the flap that allowed people in and out of the covered cart. Arissa stepped forward; she swayed because with the armor her balance was off center.

"You may need some help walking until you get used to the extra weight, but I see someone walking up, looks kind of like Kinley, he should be able to help you." Arissa smiled, she thanked the armor maker again, then left the cart, this time climbing carefully down.

The armor maker was right; Kinley was the one coming up to the cart. "I waited for you forever, just to find out that you weren't even there." He said to her before they had a chance to greet each other.

Arissa stumbled backwards as she made the short hop from the cart to the ground. Kinley made it to her in time to offer her extra support, so as not to fall. His arms felt different to her, stronger and thicker.

"Wow, that armor is beautiful. Innogen has really outdone herself this time." Arissa immediately felt a wave of shame wash over her.

This woman had made the most beautiful set of armor, specifically for her, and Arissa hadn't even bothered to commit her name to memory. *Innogen. Innogen. Innogen.* Arissa thought to herself a few times, trying to make a mental note of the armor maker's name. Arissa lifted herself out of Kinley's arms and spun around a little for him, so he was able to see all the detail in the armor.

"She put a lot of work into this. It must have taken her forever to finish." Kinley got closer to examine the breastplate taking in everything. "This bird, what is it? I don't remember hearing anything about a bird before."

"She didn't say much, I think she said maybe twenty words the whole I time I was in there. I think the Fire-Bird is what she called it." Arissa said. Kinley looked at her, confusion spread across his face. He hates not getting all the details, Arissa knew that, he had always hated not getting all the details.

"I am sure that someone knows what The Fire -Bird is," she said to him, "we may just have to ask around a little bit is all." She looked up at Kinley, the facial expressions that he showed shifted from confusion to anger, anger to irritation, and finally irritation to reluctant acceptance.

"Well," he said, "I guess it's not like we have any other choice. The answer isn't just going to fall to our feet." Kinley kicked at a few lose rocks that were sitting near his feet, as if to illustrate that there was nothing there. "Where are you off to now?" he asked her looking up.

"Well," she replied, "I was thinking that I would go over to Kieron's to see if my weapon is done yet, it's been a while since we've stopped. Do you want to come with me?"

"Yes, like I said, I've been at your tent waiting for you." All Kinley could see through the opening in the helmet was her eyes, and he could tell that something clicked in her brain.

"Oh, that's right, I am so sorry, I forgot. Can we talk as we walk though?" she asked taking a step, only to find that she wasn't used to the weight of the armor. She stumbled forward knocking into Kinleys' shoulder. Her arms waved wildly as she tried to regain her balance, only to be rescued by Kinley a split second before she would have fallen face first into the packed dirt. Kinley grabbed her shoulders in what seemed like an effortless and fluid movement, and then steadied her. He casually slid one arm though hers and motioned for her to take a step with the other. She did, and using his body for support, took her first weighted steps in her new armor.

"I guess this is going to take a little getting used to." She said nervously.

"It's okay," Kinley replied, "you should be used to it before too long."

"Yeah, but getting used to it and being able to fight in it are completely different things." She took another step.

"If you don't start putting more weight on your own body I am going to have a bruise on my arm." Kinley teased.

"Oh, give me a break," she told him, "or I won't listen when you tell me what you said you have to tell me."

"My dream." Kinley said with excitement in his voice. "I have to tell you about my dream."

"Great! Another dream, who do I have to steak through the heart this time?" Arissa said and Kinley was able to hear the smile in her voice.

"You know Arissa, you may think so, but everything is not always about you." Kinley turned his head towards her as they walked and stuck out his tongue.

"Fine, whatever, what was your dream about?" she asked slowing down a little, watching her feet as she walked. Kinley was able to feel the shift in her weight with each footstep. He excitedly went over every detail of his dream. Seeing the green fish again and the strange feeling of friendship that he had towards it, being able to feel his own touch on his face when his hand touched the reflection. He tried to explain to her what it was like to see someone you have never seen or met before and then to realize that it's you.

He told her what the Man-God looked like, and how strange it was to see someone next to you in a reflection, and then to look over and realize that no one is there. He told her of their conversation, then of the kiss that they shared. He told her about the tingling feeling that lingered on his lips after the kiss.

"… and then he said 'Even when you think I am not with you, I am. I will never leave you.'" Arissa slowed down during Kinleys description of the dream.

"Wow," she said, "that's just… intense."

"I know, but here is the thing, right. This dream, it wasn't like when I was in the memories at all. See, while I was there I was able to choose what I was going to do. This, this was completely different, I was just there, watching from inside one of the characters."

"Hmmm, well, maybe this was planned out, you know. Pre-determined." She wondered aloud now stopped with one hand on her waste and the other on the side of the Fire-Bird helmet.

"I guess…" Kinley said, but before he was able to get another word out Arissa had interrupted him.

"I guess… well, I mean, I wonder if you'd have had a choice in the matter, would you have done anything different?"

"Honestly, the thought had never occurred to me. No, I don't think I would have done a single thing different." He answered; a smile crossed his face as he remembered the feeling that danced across his lips after the kiss he shared with his love.

"Well," Arissa said, "then I would like to know why it matters. Whether you could control your choices or not, I mean." with that she started tugging at Kinley's arm, pulling him towards Kieron's' cart. He smiled at her and followed her, noticing the lack of pressure that she placed on his arm.

"Do you know what kind of weapon he is making for you?" he asked her curiously.

"No, I don't think he even knew. I actually don't think that he was planning on making me one when I jumped onto his cart."

"He is kind of a stubborn old coot, what made him change his mind?"

"Kieron? He saw me fight. Peadar was there and I kind of beat him until he couldn't move."

Kinley laughed, he added a little bit of acid in his tone and said, "I bet that he hated that."

"Not that you would know, but that wasn't the first time that I took him down." she shot back defensively, "You were too busy running around in your fantasy world."

"Ouch," he said, looking at her, "if looks could kill. You may not remember this but the last time I saw him he was saying something along the lines of 'keep your girlfriend up front with the rest of the women.' and now you talk about him like he is the greatest person that ever existed." trying to make her laugh he added, "When I am clearly the greatest person who ever existed."

For some reason she didn't find it funny, instead she looked ahead quietly, measuring the distance between their position and Kieron's cart. They walked in silence the rest of the way and when they arrived at the cart Arissa turned to him and spoke. "Wait here, I am going to go in on my own." Kinley muttered something under his breath, too low for Arissa to hear. He then boosted her up onto the cart. She turned and looked at him before entering into the covered area. She smiled and then walked in, entirely on her own. Feeling very proud of herself, she strode into the covered portion of the cart with a very smug look on her face.

Arissa was surprised when she stepped into the canvas-covered area. It was so brightly lit that her eyes stung. There were glow-grub bulbs that emitted a bluish-white light that reached everywhere, hanging from the support poles, dangling from the topside covering, and they were set flat on almost every horizontal surface. At the end of the elongated cart,

Kieron stood facing a workbench. His back was turned to her and he grumbled to himself, unaware that Arissa had even entered. She decided not to be rude by announcing her presence, and stayed back waiting for him to finish what he was doing.

She noticed that occasionally his mutterings would grow louder as he shouted things like "this piece of junk" or "why won't you fit together" and "finally, took you long enough." He would pick up tools, lean in close to whatever he was working on and mutter to himself, then put the tools back, stretch his arms high into the air and repeat the whole process over again. At one point, he picked up the object that had absorbed so much of his attention and raised it as if to throw it to the floor. Right before he thrust his arm down, he looked at it and gently lowered it back onto the workbench. He grabbed a tiny tool with a pointed end and focused intently tapping the object.

"MECHANICS" he shouted at the top of his lungs then he lowered his voice. Arissa was listening as hard as she could, but still was only to collect just the end of what he said. "…simple weapons just won't do. I should have stabbed myself right there. Just… about… FINISHED. Now where is that girl? Innogen should be done with her by now, unless Peadar screwed the message up, leave it to him that lazy lump of…" Arissa didn't give him a chance to finish what he was saying. She cleared her throat, just as she had done with Innogen.

The cranky old man turned towards her "How long have you been there?" he asked gruffly.

"I came in somewhere between 'this piece of junk' and 'MECHANICS'." she yelled the last word in mock-frustration and made it more dramatic by slamming her fist on her leg. The look on his face said all that Arissa needed to hear.

"How are you Kieron?" she asked humbling her voice to simulate a respectful tone. He didn't notice the fact that the respect in her voice was false.

He grunted a very fast "fine" to her and turned to grab the item that he was working on.

"What are mechanics?" she asked him.

"They are what make your weapon different from all the others; you see I came up with something completely new for you." He said. "You'll notice that most fighters have some form of blade, be it an axe, sword or even a knife. There are a few with range weapons like bows and arrows. You fight well enough up close, but I was curious what you would be able to do with a little distance between you and those filthy Ree-Kyae."

"When you and Peadar were in here fighting, or I should say when you beat the breath from Peadars lungs," he gave a little snicker, "anyway, you're fighting style is very fluid. I wanted to make sure that fluidity would transfer from your arm, to your weapon, but I didn't want to stick you with something that was only long range. Switching between two weapons is far too much trouble when you are surrounded by those nasty things, which is where the *mechanics* come in. You're weapon changes from hand-held to long range with the push of a button and a flick of the wrist."

"A flick of the wrist?" Arissa asked skeptically.

"Yes! A flick of the wrist. Don't you listen when people are talking to you? You are an exceptional fighter, but that doesn't make you the smartest, now does it?" he answered.

It was Arissa's turn to grunt this time, but

Kieron acted as if he didn't hear it. "I see you have your armor. Show me the right leg." Arissa twisted her leg around to show the grumpy old man the pouch that semi-wrapped around her right leg. "That's perfect!" He exclaimed, "It will fit perfectly in there. Now your arm, show me your right arm." Arissa held out her arm showing the right arm of her armor. "Good length," he said, "not as short as I'd hoped but it should still work. I see that Innogen took my semi-forceful advice about the design. Beautiful work, though I do have to say that it will pale in comparison to my weapon. Yes... Yes... nice detail on the Fire-Bird."

"The Fire-Bird, what is it?" Arissa asked, not even half expecting an answer.

"That, Arissa, is not for me to tell you. I am not a storyteller. Who knows, maybe Fallyn will break some more rules and let whoever has the misfortune to tell your questioning little mind what the Fire-Bird is also illumistrate the story for you. I, however, am the weapon maker, so my part is to give you this."

He held out his hands showing her the weapon that had constructed. At first, Arissa thought he was playing a prank on her, because what Kieron held in his hands looked almost nothing like a weapon, but more like art. It was a little longer then her forearm, and the color of fire. It definitely matched the armor that she was wearing. The metal was the same fiery orange and red combination as the raised images of the Fire-Bird on her breastplate and the pouch on her right leg. The weapon was in the shape of that bird, wings outstretched.

The beak of the bird was opened, and what looked like flame was exploding out of its mouth. The flame at the end was sharp and thin, maybe the size of her hand, fingers laid flat. The flames tapered off into five spikes that extended past the rest of the flame, two to each side and one very wicked looking one that came out of the tip that pointed downward. The same red jewel that was on her armor rested in the middle of the flame, this one was larger and seemed to be filled with moving orange sparks. She noticed that the edge of the flames looked very thin, and it hit her that the flame itself was the blade, she imagine the beautiful flame dripping with the scarlet blood of the Ree-Kyae and smiled.

Arissa took her helmet off and set it on a bench behind her. She extended her arms towards the weapon and Kieron placed it in her hands. She didn't think that it was possible, but Kieron had seemed to capture more detail and give this sculpture a life that Innogen could only have hoped to accomplish. Every feather on this Fire-Bird seemed to end in a tiny flame, giving it the appearance that if she touched it, she would burn herself. The head was shaped like her helmet and it had the same three feathers with the strange bulbous points at the tip, only all the detail seemed a little softer.

Arissa looked to her helmet and back to the head of the weapon, and noticed that the weapon held more rounded features then the helmet. This made the weapon actually look somewhat cute, and not as fierce as the helmet. Again, the glittering red jewel had been designated as the eyes of the bird; Arissa brought the bird closer to her face. The eyes seemed to hold a depth that, she felt, was unnatural. She went to pull the bird away from her face and felt a hot sensation on her cheek. Kieron bellowed a laugh and followed it with

"Looks like your weapon has already tasted its first blood, and it's your own. Wipe your face." He laughed again tossing a dirty piece of leather at her.

The leather landed on the Fire-Bird in her hands. She turned and set it next to the helmet on the bench. She noticed that the wing of the bird had something red and shining on it. It was blood, her blood. She grabbed the leather and wiped the wing, she wanted to make sure that it was clean before tending to her cheek, when she pulled the leather away from the wing she now had two pieces. "More blades?" she asked aloud to no one particular.

"Yes, more blades, this is the 'hand-to-hand' version of the weapon, the melee side of it. Do you remember how I told you I wanted it to be both range and close combat? Here not only do you have the flame-blade, but also the wings, they are sharp, as you now know, are you going to clean up your cheek?" she turned to Kieron and noticed that he had a smug smile on his face.

"Yes, I am going to clean my cheek." She pressed the leather to her face, the cut stung and the leather did a sorry job of soaking up the blood, it more smeared it then anything. Arissa turned back towards the weapon, looking directly at the wings. She could see now, they were sharp on the outer edges; the feather work was beautiful on the wings, the flight feathers tapered off to flames that seemed to fit with the overall design of the bird. The tail looked as if it was leather, but it had a very strange rigidity. Unlike on the armor there were only two feathers on the weapon, they seemed to form a loop then turned and crisscrossed each other and ended in a delicate turn.

"What is this? How did you do that?" she

asked Kieron.

"It's very, very thin metal that's been shaped and wrapped in leather, it allows for stiffness and flexibility. I am sure you would want to move your arm in battle, after all."

"How do I hold it?"

"I call this a Sleeve Weapon, it's a brand new concept that I came up with, just for you, make sure Caedmon knows that. You'll notice that your arm fits in a cavity under the Fire-Bird, there is a bar at the end, you grab onto that and as you are tightly holding the bar your arm flex's, so there is no chance of the weapon slipping or sliding. When it's in 'melee' mode you have the three blades, the two on the wings and the one locked into the mouth, you can slash back and forth with the wing blades or you can punch forward with the flame-blade, you can even use the hooked spike at the tip of the flame blade to disembowel your target." Kieron explained.

"You keep saying 'ranged' and 'melee' how do I switch between the two? Or I should ask, what's the difference between the two?" Arissa asked.

"The difference between the two is that you can use this same weapon for long range, or ranged attacks. There is a thick, and very tough, coil of braded leather inside your weapon; the leather is also attached to the flame-blade that is coming out of the beak of the Fire-Bird. At the end of the bar, I told you about, the one that you hold onto, there is a raised area, and you'll be able to feel it. You press that down and then flip your wrist outward, then release the raised area and any slack will be retracted back into the weapon, that way the leather won't be in your way the whole fight. Now when you're not using it," he said, arm pointing to Arissa's leg, "it should fit right in that pouch, flame-blade down. That gives you fast access to it, you just reach your arm down into the pouch through the flexible metal straps and grab the bar, then bring it right out. You're going to need some practice fighting with it, but that's why Peadar's here."

"Peadar's here?" he asked turning around and lookingtowards the flap.

"Not in here, he is waiting for you outside; I had him set up a temporary training field while we are stopped, "Now, let's see how it fits on your arm. Hold out your right arm."

Arissa did, now she understood why the armor only covered half of her right arm, the Fire-Bird covered the lower half. She pushed her arms in the flexible leather wrapped metal and kept pushing her arm forward. She reached the bar that Kieron had spoken of and grabbed hold of it. Her arm automatically flexed when she gripped and she understood what he meant about the weapon not sliding. It seemed that while she was holding on to the bar the muscles in her arm bulged and the fit was very snug.

"Wow, it's not as heavy as I thought it would be." Arissa said.

"Of course it's not; it's true that most of my weapons are heavy, but not this one. You had to be able to lift it as well as keep your speed and agility. I guess that's not Innogen's style, but you'll get used to the extra weight."

"Thank you for the weapon Kieron." She said, wanting to leave and make her way out to Peadar.

"You'd better be, it wasn't easy to come up with that thing, and it definitely wasn't easy to get it done as soon as I did. Remember to tell Caedmon everything that I told you." He said.

Arissa didn't know what else to say, she was thankful but for some reason she felt like she needed to elaborate. She was happy when Kieron turned around and repetitively flopped his hand back and forth in the air towards her, apparently waving her away. She slid the weapon into her pouch on her right leg, letting go of the bar she was gripping, her muscles relaxed and her arm slid right out of the sleeve and the weapon fit perfectly into the metal pouch. She picked her helmet up, pulled it onto her head and turned to face the flap. She stepped outside trying to regain her balance as her body swayed from over calculating the distance. She looked down and noticed that, as Kieron had said, Peadar was there waiting for her, he looked awkwardly down to his feet as Kinley played with his own fingers.

"So I am guessing that you guys want to see this thing?" she grabbed hold of the pole and slid down a little faster than she was comfortable. Her feet hit the hard ground and pain shot through her knees, ignoring it she stepped over to where the boys were.

"Hi Peadar." She said in greeting, both Peadar and Kinley looked up at her once they heard her voice. She felt their eyes sweep over her searching for the weapon that Kieron had just given to her.

"Hey Arissa." he said, eyes still scanning to try to locate this new weapon. Unlike Kinley, Peadar had been in the cart with Arissa when she had her first meeting with Kieron, so he knew that Kieron wasn't just going to make her a sword or a bow and arrows, but something completely different.

She could tell that he didn't want to be rude by

asking to see it, but the frantic bobbing that his head was doing as his eyes searched her body for it wasn't exactly polite. Arissa saw Kinley's eyes shoot over to him and a look of confusion came across his face.

He looked at Arissa, "So where is this super special amazing weapon that Kieron made for you?" he asked, directly. Arissa smiled, she had known Kinley for far too long for him to worry about pleasantries with her.

Arissa stood on the toe of her right leg, remaining flatfooted on her left and twisted inward showing them the pouch on her right thigh with the firebird across it, "It's in here."

Now it was Peadar's turn to have a confused look on his face. Arissa chuckled and reached into the pouch and felt for the bar, its position seemed to come natural to her. She grabbed hold of it and pulled out the brightly polished Fire-Bird.

"That's a weapon?" Peadar asked the confusion that showed on his face now audible, "How is that statue a weapon?"

From inside the cart Arissa heard a grunt followed by the word "idiot" being muttered softly.

"It's beautiful, isn't it?" she said turning toward Kinley, intentionally ignoring Peadars question.

"Yes, it is. Did Kieron beat you up in there? Your face is bleeding?" he answered her, pointing to the spot on her cheek that she had cut with the wing of the Fire-Bird.

Arissa laughed, answering his question with "No, this little baby just has more blades on it then I was aware of. I can't wait to test it out."

"You mean that cute little bird can actually draw blood?" Peadar teased, which, in turn, made Arissa angry.

"Yeah, it can draw blood, why don't you come over here and pet its pretty wing, then you'll see."

"Wow, calm down She-Kyae, I was just joking with you," he said, stunned at how much offence she had taken to his banter, "besides, I am the one that's been working since he woke up to construct a training ground for you. If Kieron made it, then it has to be good, I want to see the damage it can do."

"Well," Kinley said, "if that's the case then... uhhh... I think I am going leave you two be. I have some stuff I need to do anyway."

"Are you sure Kinley?" Arissa asked him, he still hadn't seen her fight and she wanted to show him the way that the weapon switched but she could tell that he was uncomfortable being there.

"Yeah I am sure, you'll have to show me later," He smiled at her, "and honestly I would rather you have a little practice with that thing before I was around you with it. You already cut your face, how long until mine's the next target?"

She put the Fire-Bird into the pouch on her leg and embraced Kinley, the she watched as he walked away, leaving her and Peadar standing alone by the cart.

"So, what does this training ground you built me have?" Arissa asked Peadar as they walked past cart's and tents.

"There are some dummies," Peadar said, "and don't think it's too creepy, but Fallyn wanted me to put some of the Ree-Kyae corpses up from the battle, so you could feel what it's like for your weapon to actually strike them, that and the materials for the dummies are sort of difficult to come by, so it's mainly dead Ree-Kyae."

"You mean I have to slice open some dead things?" she asked, feeling a little nauseous, "Isn't that disrespectful or something?"

"It would be if I had put our fighters up, the burning is taking place when everyone wakes up," he said, "and those creatures don't deserve that so they'll just be left out. No respect for life, no respect in death."

The burning, Arissa thought, *I guess it's time for everyone to say goodbye to those who were lost in battle.* The more she thought about the Varians who died the angrier she got at the Ree-Kyae, the more okay she was with using their corpses for battle practice and soon any nauseous feelings she had about disemboweling their dead bodies had past.

"We haven't had a burning in a while." Arissa said, almost forgetting what it was.

"Yeah, but we also haven't had a battle in a while." Peadar said looking at his feet.

Arissa looked out into the darkness; her face was pointed in the direction where she knew the bodies of the Varians lay. She could picture them lined up and wrapped in incense soaked colored cloth, their weapons lying on top of the colored mounds. She could already see the children in their mothers arms crying as their fathers and brothers were burned, each of them having placed something of meaningat the foot of the bodies of their loved ones. Anger flooded her even more then it had before, she was ready to practice, she was ready for the Ree-Kyae to attack again, and ready to introduce them to her new Fire-Bird weapon. Even more importantly, she was ready to die so that the others could be safe and well protected from these monsters.

Chapter Six

The Fire-Bird

Arissa stood looking over the training ground that Peadar had created. There were poles in the shape of a circle and hanging from those poles were some of the biggest glow-grub bottles that she had ever seen, they casted their pale blue light in every direction, illuminating a large portion of the surrounding area. At the very center of the training ground was a large fire that Peadar had built as well. There were only three dummies between the fire and the poles holding the glow-grub bottles, as well as nine Ree-Kyae corpses, all of which were strung up on polls, Peadar had even raised their arms and legs, posing them as if they were running at her. It was clear that rigor mortis had passed in the time since the battle.

"You're not going to be able to see this well in

any battle with the Ree-Kyae, but I figured that since this is your first time using your weapon you would want to see how it reacted to your movements."

Arissa nodded in understanding, then she noticed one of the figures in the area move. Limping out from behind one of the Ree-Kyae corpses came Caedmon. "Oh, I was going to go looking for him." She spoke aloud to herself. Peadar looked confused; he hadn't seen his grandfather stepping out from behind one of the stinking Ree-Kyae. Arissa bolted right to him, forgetting all that Peadar had done to arrange the training ground.

The question of what the Fire-Birds story was had been on her mind since she had seen her armor, now she wanted the answer. Peadar ran after her, finally catching sight of Caedmon, he slowed to a walk. When Arissa got to him, she didn't even have a chance to speak "I heard that you would be looking for me." He said, making a seat for himself on the ground by the fire in the center and leaning his walking stick on his shoulder. "Sit girl, and tell me what you want."

"The Fire-Bird," Arissa asked still standing, making more of a statement out of her question, "I want to know what it is. First, I was ignored then I was told to ask a storyteller. Can you tell me what it is?"

Caedmon looked past her, his face contemplative. Peadar made his way up behind Arissa, "She wants to know of the Fire-Bird. What do you think?" Caedmon said, his eyes weren't focused on anyone in the immediate area. "Sure…" Peadar said leaving it open-ended, Arissa jumped unaware that he had followed her. Caedmon reached to his waste where the little leather pouch holding the golden dust hung, he opened it and asked the question again, never looking away from the spot in the darkness that he was focused on.

Arissa understood now, he wasn't asking her or Peadar, he was consulting the dust. Everything went silent and the world around them lit up brighter then Arissa had ever seen it while she was conscious, his hand slid into the pouch. No sounds from around them penetrated their ears, yet she felt as if her senses were heighted and everything that touched them was amplified tenfold. Caedmon spoke again.

His voice was more clear and had more depth than she had ever heard, it seemed to vibrate in her ears and throughout her body as he asked "and him?" to no one who was visible. Finally, he pulled his hand out of the pouch; Arissa noticed that not even a single granule of dust clung to his hand. Her senses seemed to numb, somehow she felt cheated as Caedmon re-tied the drawstrings and re-fastened it to his waste and looked at the two of them.

"Don't tell anyone that I just did that with you two around, Arissa you will get your answers, the dust has given me the okay, and that holds a higher rank then even Fallyn."

Arissa smiled and Peadar took a seat next to her, they both impatiently waited for Caedmon to begin the tail of the Fire-Bird. He took a deep breath, still sitting next to the fire, his walking stick leaning against his shoulder, closed his eyes, and then he began to speak.

"The Fire-Bird was the one to bring fire to us. Before it, fire was angry, greedy and unwilling to work with us. It ravenously tore through anything near it, an animal more than an element. The angry rage of fire was always respected, but never regarded as highly as it is now. This was long before The Crystal Heart was high atop its perch and even longer from its shattering."

"There was only one color to this flame, black, no light from it cut through the darkness, it was an invisible and silent killer. The ash that it left behind was different as well, once the fire had abandoned it the ash was completely cool to the touch. No embers stayed back to blow in the wind and give birth to new flame. The Trading Post then was as it is now, the center of our civilization, where the five rivers meet."

Arissa was fully enveloped in the story; she pictured what Caedmon was describing in her mind's eye. The fire seemed to take shape after shape of all the animals of Arathia that had been described to her. She saw black fish swimming in and out of black waters, their black teeth gnashed as they came down on anything in their path.

She noticed once that the fire even took the shape of the Ree-Kyae. She found it strange to see their normally white and pearlescent skin a bottomless black as they ran along the earthen ground of Arathia. She saw this dark ever-changing mass in the foreground, in the background was the Trading Post, Arissa found that she was instantly afraid for the people who were there.

"The only difference was that Varians from all around Arathia set up permanent living around the Trading Post figuring that there was safety in numbers, shop keepers and traders had permanent businesses. The Trading Post was heavily guarded; swordsman with shields and archers were placed in a circle around the residents that surrounded the Trading Post to keep the Ree-Kyae at bay, and they did a good job of it. The permanent residents as well as those visiting the Trading Post had a leader; and her position came as a shock to most."

"Her name was Aislin and she was the first female ever to hold the position of leader, she was also the one with the largest group to lead. The grand counsel liked to test Aislin, which is why she had the most difficult place, as well as the largest group of people, to lead. Most felt that she would fail in her task, but Aislin was adamant to show that she wouldn't, and through her stubbornness she became one of the greatest leaders of all time."

"She had gone through many tests, but none as great as when the fire came. Looming unknown in the distance, the fire was seemingly stalking the Trading Post. A slight scent of scorched earth rose to the noses of the guards, but nothing looked out of place in the darkness. No smoke rose, no flame could be seen, but it rolled along the ground waiting to devour its prey."

"A few of the guards grabbed the glow-grub bottle from their belts and held it high, trying to illuminate as much of the area as possible, but the silent fire was too far out to be seen in the dim light. They lowered their bottles back to their belts and shot concerned looks to each other; the nervous shuffling of feet could be heard throughout the ranks of men. They didn't know what was coming, but they could tell that it was something terrible."

"Aislin noticed the scent in the air from the center of the Trading Post. She started watching and noticed the people around her looking about; puzzlement was showing on their faces. She knew what they smelled, it was the same bitter-dry stench that she did."

"She started walking, letting her nose lead the way. She passed by carts and huts of each merchant selling their goods, not paying enough attention to notice what they were selling. As she walked the stench got stronger and stronger, the world passed by faster as she broke into a jog, the merchants' carts seemed to blur by in a whirl of color, each blending into the one before it."

"She eventually passed the carts and huts leading into the settlement part of the Trading Post. People watched her as she raced passed, a look of astonishment on their faces. She waved her hand back and told the people to gather at the center of the Trading Post. They listened to her, not knowing what was wrong; Aislin herself didn't even know that the ravenous hunger of the wild fire was looming not very far from the Trading Post. She passed group after group, family after family, all of them going to opposite way, the word had spread, and she could feel that something was very wrong. "

"She finally made it to the men that were circling the Trading Post encampment; they stood there, staring out into the blackness. There was barely any movement, occasionally one of them would shuffle their feet but even that was oddly quiet. The only sound that she could hear was a faint hiss, and the deep inhale and exhalation from the men standing around her. 'Is it the Ree-Kyae?' she asked, there was no reply from the men, they stood still, like ghosts, their senses dead to the world. Aislin turned back towards the Trading Post, then back to the men. She walked to the closest one and waved her hand in front of his face, he didn't say a word, instead he just blinked, and then his eyes scrunched together as if he was trying to focus on something."

"Aislin looked down at his belt, the only source of light were the glow-grubs. She grabbed the bottle from his belt and pulled it to her face peering deep inside the little bottle. 'Glow-grub', she said, 'are normally still, barely any detectable movement. These are moving more wildly and glowing more brightly then I've ever seen.' Still watching the little worms, she noticed something in the reflection of the bottle. A black mass, separate from the darkness, was coming towards her. She looked up from the bottle, nothing could be seen, and she felt was an eerie calm deep inside. She shivered and continued to watch the translucent bottle where the glow-grub were being housed. She watched as the amorphous black mass advanced toward them. She jerked her head up, still watching the bottle, the blob slowed almost to a halt."

"She lowered her head back to the bottle, and the black mass gained speed again. 'Men,' she said, 'I don't want to alarm you, but something is approaching.' The men didn't move, they kept their eyes peeled to the front. She raised her voice, 'MEN!' The man closest to her snapped out of his daze and growled in a way that none would expect a person to sound. The others turned to face the one who growled, keeping the same distance from each other. Aislin spoke again, 'Men,' she said, something is coming at us, a dark mass that is changing shape, I can't tell the shapes, I can't see it clearly but I don't think it's the Ree-Kyae. I think it's something else, I think it's the wild fire."

"She didn't know what to expect from the men, at least a gasp, but no sound came forth. Instead, they stared intently at her, expecting orders to flee. 'I know no one has ever beaten the wild fire,' she said, 'but there has to be a way. This Trading Post is the center of our way of life, the housings around it are the homes of many Varians, and we can't let anything take that stability away from us. There are a handful of us, and we don't know how far the wild fire is surrounding, and if we try to evacuate we could end up sending our people directly into the wild fire, so we will defeat it.' Aislin was attempting the impossible; she was determined to beat something that no one else had ever been able to defeat. Determination shone in her eyes as she spoke to the men, and when she finished her speech she rattled off for the leaders of the current posted guards to come forward to her, leaving out the grand council all together."

"Once assembled, they began discussing all they knew about the wild fire. 'It has never been beaten.' one of the guards said, pacing back and forth over a trail that had been laid out of smooth stones. 'Well,' Aislin said, 'what else do we know about it? Do we know how it was formed? Is it alive? It sure acts as if it is. Is there anything that slows it down, there has got to be something that we can do to stop it.' she looked around at each of the four men standing before her, one of them even went so far as to roll his eyes at her questions. She lowered her head and closed her eyes, breathing deeply. She took a moment to gather herself, and then raised her head. Aislin didn't want to let the men get to her; she had been dealing with them looking down on her since she obtained her title. She exhaled and continued to speak 'It's true that every attempt, up until now, has failed, but we have to remember that not every option out there has been exhausted. There have been many things that have proven most difficult for many Varians, but eventually someone did end them.' Aislin had a look of pure determination, she had changed stature, she was no longer Varian, she was a force of Arathia."

Caedmon wiped the sweat from his forehead, glancing at the dirt underneath him; he was silent, as if he was listening for where the story picked up. "The Fire-Bird," he said, "That's where I was going with this. The Fire-Bird. I am an old man now, telling a story takes a lot out of me." Arissa looked to Peadar, he smiled at her, it was clear that pride for his grandfather shone through him. Arissa didn't say a word; she looked back to Caedmon and waited patiently for him to resume the story. Finally, after what seemed an eternity, he lifted his head and began to speak again.

"Whatever Aislin had said this time seemed to breathe some sense into the men. They sat around discussing battle strategy, possible weaknesses that the wild fire might have, at one point one of them even suggested feeding the wild fire until it grew too large and exploded. The wild fire grew closer and closer to the Trading Post as they spoke, its lightless licking flames grew hungrier and hungrier for the physical feast that stood before it. The guards started calling, Aislin and the others came running, still no clear battle plan had been formed. She ordered the guards surrounding the perimeter to fall back; there was no way to fight it. She didn't want to admit that the wild fire had won, that the very center of our culture was going to be destroyed and all under her command. Mostly she didn't want to admit that everyone had been right about her, she picked up dirt, throwing it at the wild fire in desperation, but to no avail. The fire kept advancing, leaving cold black ash in its path. She felt something growing inside of her, a bright red rage; it grew when she thought of the fire, the men that had always told her that she would never succeed, toward the four guard commanders who had just mocked her. The rage grew until it completely devoured her. Her fingers were bleeding, she was still clawing at the dirt, throwing it at the black fire, but it only seemed to grow. They moved back as the flame advanced it was now engulfing the tents and buildings in its path."

"Out of the corner of her eye she saw movement, but it didn't sway her, she was still filled with rage, a string of obscenities rushed from her lips. She cursed the fire, the leaders of other tribes; she cursed every man and woman that had ever wronged her. It seemed as though nothing could drag her out of the anger that had taken over her. Red flooded her vision, she could hear a pounding in her ears, the nubs of her fingers bled profusely as they scraped against rock and dirt, and she looked like one of the Ree-Kyae as she fought in desperation to hold back the wild fire. Paying little attention to that movement, her anger grew, she was now hissing and spitting at the wild fire, the others around her watched obviously afraid of the woman and the situation that they were in. Something pulled at the back of her mind, at that moment her head jerked to the side and she snapped out of her rage."

"A child, very young, was running toward the wild fire, curiosity in his eyes. Everything happened in an instant, Aislin wasn't able to control her movement, she darted towards the child, scooping him up in her arms and pulling him close to her. She heard a snap and felt warm liquid rushing down her leg; she tried to stand, but collapsed. The men watched, just staring at her, and not moving. She screamed, not out of pain, but out of distress and they seemed to snap out of whatever was holding onto them. One ran to the child in her arms and scooped him up, two others were following to pick her up and drag her out of the wild fires path, but the flame was already there, licking at her leg, a tinge of red started to run through the black flames as the fire touched the blood-soaked earth."

"The red spread and intensified, and where it was brightest, the flame started to die out. Heat started radiating from the fire, as did light; everything could be seen around them. Aislin looked at her leg, able to see the injury, she expected nothing to be left, the black flame had touched it, and nothing is left after the black flame touches. Instead, her leg was whole, the bone was showing through her shin from where she broke it, and the skin of her leg had been charred. She felt a new pain; one that no one else had ever felt, her skin was burned. She felt the stinging run up her leg, felt heat radiating off it, and it hurt her, but she smiled, the flame was dying out and she was the first one to beat it. The shapes that had been forming and changing throughout the black flame turned red and shrunk back, all of them to a center point."

"The last creature that the flame had been was like one never seen before by any Varian. A bird, dark and menacing, a crest on the top of its head that smoldered as the bird turned from black to bright red. As color took over the creature, the bird became beautiful, majestic even. It shrunk in shape, but didn't completely disappear, instead the, now red, bird flew off, made completely of the new flame. That Bird, Arissa, is the one that's engraved into your armor, and the flame that made that bird up was the black flame, the wild fire. It changed into the flame that we know now, Aislin had tamed it, many people think her blood satiated the wild hunger of that damned creature, but that's not what happened at all."

"Her sacrifice, or would be sacrifice, partnered with the life giving fluid is what changed the fire, the pure anger that had possessed her, followed by the pure terror for the child, followed by the love for the child, all these emotions were pure in her. There was no underlying motive or emotion, and that is what changed the flame, you see, it was all still in her blood when the wild fire tasted it and, mixed with the mysterious life giving properties of blood, gave the black flame a new life."

Arissa waited for Caedmon to say more, but nothing more left his lips. She looked at Peadar and, guessed by the expression on his face, that this story was new to him. Her eyes moved back to Caedmon, "So what does this have to do with me, this Fire-Bird thing?"

He hmm'd and uhhh'd before answering, "Arissa, you are the first of your kind. You are a female fighter, and a damn good one at that. You are opening a new doorway for everyone and, though you don't know it yet, whatever you do will change how absolutely everything is seen."

Arissa looked at Caedmon, her mouth hung agape. She tried to speak but her mouth felt too dry. Peadar looked at her, waiting for her to say something, the shock showed on his face as well. Caedmon sat patiently, he expected this reaction from both of them, and he looked satisfied that his assumption was correct.

"That's… that's…" Peadar didn't know what to say, "We should get started on your battle training…" he trailed off intentionally, trying to move onto something else, and deliver Arissa from the shock. Her eyes still darted back and forth, almost automatically; she blinked a few times and snapped back to reality. "Yeah… training."

Chapter Seven

Training

Arissa stepped back taking in the sight of the dimly illuminated training field around her with new respect, she stuck her hand into the pouch on her thigh. She grasped the metal bar of her weapon and felt her forearm tighten, locking the weapon into place. It felt good to her, like it was always there and would always be there.

No training needed, she thought to herself as she lifted her arm out of the pouch, Fire-Bird glistening in the glow-grub light. Arissa swung her arm up and snapped it around to her side; she pressed the small button on the side of the bar within the weapon, which released the blade. It flung out away from her then snapped back. It rushed towards her head, grazing her cheek. Blood dripped from the fresh cut and rolled down her face, her hair sopped most of it up when it reached her jaw line.

The dark red dripped onto the metal of her armor and rolled to the leather, the spot on the leather darkened as the blood soaked in. The blade was sucked back into the weapon, locking into place at the beak of the Fire-Bird. "Well," said Peadar, "I guess it's a good thing that you didn't cut your leg off or lose a finger." He chuckled and winked at her, then added, "You should try your melee combat before you move onto ranged with a weapon like that."

"Melee?" she asked him.

"It's basically close range fighting." he clarified. Pushing her slightly towards one of the dummies that had been propped up. "I just want you to act like you're punching it, then go ahead and get a little more creative with the way you slash at it."

Arissa took an anxious step towards the dummy; she looked to the side at one of the illuminated Ree-Kyae bodies, and then moved towards it. "No!" Peadar yelled, "Those are for the long range attacks. You don't want to be up close to one of those when its intestines come spilling out at you, if you think the outside stinks, you should wait until you get a good whiff of the insides."

"Oh," said Arissa, "I didn't think about that, I guess it makes sense that if they smell like they're rotting when they're alive, then you definitely don't want to smell them dead." She turned back toward the dummy and started walking to it. She punched at it with the blade and felt it sink into something soft and squishy. "What's in here?" she asked, "I expected it to be stuffed with dried moss, like from the mattresses."

"Well, it is not." said Peadar; "I wanted it to at

least feel semi-real so I stuffed it with some of the fish insides from the last meal." it was then that she noticed the smell. "Well, go crazy on it." Peadar told her, and he was not disappointed. Arissa started on it as he had always seen her fight. She ducked, then thrusted the blade that was attached to her fist into the dummy repeatedly. She pretended that the dummy was striking back at her as she bobbed in and out dealing killing blow after killing blow, slashing at its throat, chest and straight through the head. She made her way around every inch of the dummy until all that hung on the pole were a few scraps of torn fabric and a pile of minced fish guts lay on the ground under it.

"There was honestly no doubt in my mind that you would be great at the melee fighting, but the ranged is going to take some getting used to." Peadar said as he noticed that she was breathing heavily. He pulled out a waterskin and offered it to her, "Have some water, then sit for a little bit and we'll start on the corpses." She nodded gratefully and stuck the weapon back into the pouch on her leg, releasing the bar and letting it rest on the bottom. She then grabbed the waterskin and drank; still drinking she crossed her legs and sat.

She got her fill of water then handed it back to Peadar, who was watching her. "You tire out to quickly." he said. She glared at him, "only for now." she said, "you just wait until I get used to it, then we'll see who tires out first. Besides I don't have to last a long time if I only have to cause a little bit of damage to take something down." for the first time since hearing Caedmon's story, she had noticed that he wasn't in sight, she expected him to be here watching her, picking up details about her training for his story.

"Where did your grandfather go?" she asked.

"Oh, he said that stories about heroines training aren't told well. He also said that he would find you when we were done here. Besides, I think he had a meeting with Fallyn, since we're so close to the Trading Post and everything that happened with the Ree-Kyae. He's been meeting a lot with Fallyn since the attack"

Arissa stopped responding to Peadar and noticed how tired her body was. The muscles in her legs had just started to burn from the movement of trying to out-step the dummy, her face was throbbing from both the earlier cut and the one she had just obtained. She took a moment to stretch before standing back up. She glanced at Peadar, and even in the dim light of the glow-grub bottles, could see him watching her.

She reached her hand back into the pouch on her thigh and grasped the bar of the weapon. "Now, when using this you want to think of it even more as an extension of your arm. Any move that your arm makes, so will the blade; it will just take a little bit longer. That's something that you have to get used to, timing is everything in a fight. Also, you really don't want to make any sudden movements with your arm without thinking how it's going to affect your blade, that's what happened with your face, well, one side anyway."

Arissa just looked at him as she pulled the weapon out of the pouch on her leg. "Well, you may want to stand back then, because I clearly am unaware of how to work this thing." she said to him, her eyes were threatening but her smile showed that she was joking. Peadar took a step back as Arissa took a few steps toward one of the corpses; she whipped her hand back and then forward, pressing the little button on the side. The flame blade shot out of the beak of the Fire-Bird and sailed through the air towards the corpse. She pulled her hand back at just the right moment. The blade caressed the stomach of the Ree-Kyae just enough to slice through the skin. Entrails spilled out onto the ground beneath it but Arissa wasn't finished. She waved her hand over her head in a circle and thrust it back out, the blade followed sailing through the air slicing clean through the Ree-Kyae's neck. Its head tipped on its side as if still connected, then rolled to the ground. The blade was still sailing through the air, Arissa flicked her arm up into the air and the blade followed until it was straight above her. She pressed the button on the side and the blade came back down towards her and locked into place in the beak once more.

"Okay," she said, "I really, really like that part of this weapon."

"Kieron has definitely outdone himself with this one." Peadar said still staring at Arissa.

It was then that the smell reached them, the normal smell of decay that accompanied the Ree-Kyae was nothing compared to how they smelled on the inside. Arissa's eyes started watering, her nose burned and her gag reflex instantly kicked in. Peadar wasn't in much better shape, within moments they were both doubled over retching. Peadar had already thought of what to do, nine holes were dug near each corpse with a large pile of dirt next to them. He drug himself closer in between the bouts of sickness that struck him and eventually worked the remainder of the corpse into the hole. Moreover, after retching one more time he pushed the mound of dirt. The smell dissipated and they scraped up some dirt to cover their vomit.

"Next time, let's make sure we do that part a little faster," Arissa said wiping her mouth, "I don't remember them smelling that bad during the fight."

"They've been laying there for a while," Peadar told her, "and the smell of death intensifies almost immediately with them." Peadar wiped his mouth as well, then smiled weakly and asked, "Are you ready to do it all over again?"

Arissa thought about it for a moment, the stench of the Ree-Kyae had barely left her nostrils, she wasn't sure she wanted to ever smell anything that putrid again, and definitely not so soon, but Fallyn had kept them from moving on until she was semi-trained on her weapon.

"Honestly?" she asked, "No, but I have no choice, we have to get on to the Trading Post and we can't do that until I'm finished with this." Arissa stood up and got to work on the other two dummies and eight corpses, she ran from corpse to dummy and back and forth, attacking them in no logical order. She dodged invisible blows and used combination range and melee attacks on every body, no matter if it was a corpse or a dummy, and each blow that she dealt would have left the enemy either immobile, unconscious or dead.

Peadar followed behind her, he held his breath as he shoved bits, pieces, and scraps of the Ree-Kyae into holes with a flattened stick. When all the parts and pieces of the Ree-Kyae were cleaned up Arissa and Peadar went to work on deconstructing the training field. The Poles that made up the supports were pulled from the ground and bundled up, wood was far too valuable to be left behind, no matter how bad it smelled. Peadar propped the bundle on his shoulder and left the fire burning. Arissa followed him to the carts; he moved the bundle from his shoulder over the side of the cart. The bundle crashed to the floor, it was obviously heavier then Arissa thought Peadar made it look. A sticky sweet smell drifted up her nostrils. Incense again, "The burning, it must be happening right now." Peadar said, his nostrils flared as he sniffed at the air.

He took off in a run and Arissa followed as they wove their way back through the carts and tents to the battlefield. By the time they reached the burning the flame had started on one end of the fallen fighters and was making its way to the other in a wave of procession. Fallyn had already said his speech and the families were standing at the head side of each body. No one made a sound as the fire spread from body to body, sweet smoke rose into the air and the fire crackled.

The flame burned itself out and a pile of ashes was left in its place. Smoke no longer rose into the air and the Varians standing around the piles of ash had started to dissipate, leaving the grieving families standing by themselves. Arissa and Peadar left in separate directions, she wanted to catch up to Kinley, wherever he was. Before heading out to find him she stopped off at her family tent to drop off her armor and her weapon and change her clothes, she still smelled like a decaying Ree-Kyae. As she removed her pants, she felt something stiff in her back pocket. She reached in and pulled out the leather wrapped package that contained her shard of The Crystal Heart. She set it aside and continued clothes, grabbing it as she headed out the flap.

She raced to Keeva's tent, thinking that Kinley would be there, but no one was outside. The fire was still roaring so she sat by it for a moment, trying to think of where he could be. She waited, fingers rapped on her leg, back and forth. She heard footsteps and turned to see Kinley walking into the firelight with one of the monsters from the river in his hands. Keeva and Enat were following behind him, each holding a small jar filled with something white. Kinley smiled at Arissa, she returned the smile but it didn't reach her eyes. Kinley knew that she was holding back a little bit of resentment towards him, and probably because he had just been murdered because of one of those monsters.

"Hey Arissa, didn't expect to see you here. Would you like to eat with us? Ma and Keeva got some new stuff from Caedmon to put on the fish." he told her.

"Thank you, I will, and I've had it before." she said shortly feeling the shard digging into her leg. "I need to give you something though." she looked at the fish that he held in his hand. Serrated fins climbed from the top of its head to its tail as well as along the sides of its body. It was a sickly green color aside from the fins themselves, which lit up and flashed in fluorescent blue, blood was still pumping throughout the fish's body. Its teeth weren't as bad as she expected them to be, short stubby little things that came to a dull point.

"Can it wait until after we eat," he asked, "I've got to get the poison sack out of this thing before it bursts and the poison spreads to the meat."

"Yeah, sure." she said not wanting to compromise the safety of the people around her.

Kinley set the fish down and grabbed the

sharpened stone that he used to gut and clean the fish. After it was cleaned and the poison sack was safely removed, he filleted it and moved them to the flat stones that were heated on the fire. Arissa pulled on his arm; he looked over and saw Enat and Keeva fussing over the fish, white powdery flakes being sprinkled onto it. Kinley stood up and allowed himself to be pulled away.

Once they were alone, Arissa reached into her pocket and pulled out the leather wrapped shard. "I thought you should have this." she said handing it to him.

"What is it? Is that my…" he trailed off and his hand moved to his back pocket, he was comforted when he felt the now familiar shape of his love. "What is it?" he corrected.

"I found it while you were… out. I didn't want to ruin yours so I used this one, but I figured that you should have it since I kept it to replace the one that I thought you threw away." she said looking sheepishly at the ground.

"There's something I have to tell you." he said, "I think you should know that I don't think I am going to be walking with everyone for much longer."

"What do you mean?" she asked, "Where are you going?"

"I have to find the rest of these, it's my job. Do you remember the story we used to listen in on, Caedmon and his telling of how The Crystal Heart was shattered? Well, it turns out that the man who shattered it was my father. Only I can restore it back to what it once was."

"Wait that would make…. Enat… the woman?" she asked.

"Yes, but the point is that I have to collect all the other pieces and I have to put them back together."

Arissa looked contemplative "Okay, when do we leave."

"We?" Kinley asked. "Who's we, Arissa you are a fighter now, you have a weapon and armor, you can't go with me, you have responsibilities here. Besides what about Peadar, you two seemed to be getting along… well."

"I'll figure something out, I didn't stab you and kill you to bring you back to life just to have you leave again you know." she told Kinley, her face adopted a stern look.

Kinley spoke one word, the look on his face said everything and seemed to give more power to that word then any following it could. "No." His voice was calm and definite, ending any argument. Still something lingered in Arissa's eyes that concerned him. She watched the glowing cyan flecks in his eyes through the darkness and looked away.

"I really need something else to carry these in." he said, changing the subject. He reached into his back pocket and pulled out his shard. "I can't be walking around with a pocket full of these things. I'm going to end up getting hurt by them one of these days."

"Kinley, you of all people should know better than that, even if you did get hurt, you'd be healed instantly, you should ask The Crystal Heart why that happens."

"I think that I already have an idea as to why that happens, but maybe I'll ask to confirm it." Kinley replied as he placed both shards into his back pocket. "Why did you bring me away to give this to me?" he asked her.

"Well, I didn't know if I should give it to you in front of Enat and Keeva, it's kind of a special thing, don't you think? It's not like everyone has a piece of The Crystal Heart laying around."

"Yeah, you're right, sorry that I didn't think of that before." Kinley said giving her a hug. "Thank you for the shard, I appreciate it, now do you mind if we go back to eat, I'm starting to get kind of hungry."

Kinley watched as Arissa hung her head in defeat and walked back to the fire. Either Keeva or Enat had removed the flaky grey meat of the fish from the fire, the two of them were eating their fill as Kinley and Arissa walked over. They sat, silently and grabbed a piece of fish and started eating. Kinley was surprised at how the fish tasted, it wasn't the normal bland fish, this fish had depth to the taste of it. He quickly finished what he was eating and then reached out for some more. Once his hunger was sated, he noticed almost a buzzing in his back pocket. It seemed to him that the pulsating of the shards had intensified only just a little.

He, Arissa, Keeva and Enat sat by the fire after eating, enjoying the feeling of fullness, there was now water boiling over the heat, a couple full waterskins sat next to Kinley, the rest were empty and lay in wait. Kinley looked at Enat, she was rubbing her forearm again, where Kinley suspected the shard of The Crystal Heart was resting. He wondered if she had felt the pulsation that he did. He wondered if the strange movement of force had intensified for her when he brought his shard closer, and if it was even stronger now that he had two shards resting in his back pocket. Even more so, he wondered if she was hurting because of the shard, wondered if every day she felt a stabbing pain in her arm as he did in his chest when Arissa had stabbed him.

He seemed to zone out as his mind focused on the spot that his mother was rubbing, eventually thinking he could see a white glow through her skin. Enat stopped rubbing her arm "Kinley is there a reason you are watching me so intently?" she asked him, he heard her but wasn't listening to what she said. His eyes were fixed on the spot on her arm and the white light that he imagined seemed to start pulsating to the beat of the shards in his pocket, each beat causing it to grow brighter. Enat tried getting his attention a few more times but found herself failing at each attempt until, finally, Arissa reached over, shoving his shoulder.

"Hey!" He said, "What'd you do that for?" he had almost fallen over from her touch.

"What in Arathia is wrong with you?" she asked him, "You're mother has been trying to get your attention.

"I… uhhh… nothing. Sorry." he said, blinking his eyes a couple of times, noticing that each time he did the glowing spot on his mother's arm darkened.

"You had me worried for a moment, you looked like you were going to jump from where you're sitting and rip my arm off." Enat said moving her hand to the spot where the shard was kept safe, as if hiding it from Kinley. She chuckled, trying to shove off the creepy feeling that she felt "You've been through quite a bit though, I suspect that you're tired?" she asked him.

"No Ma, not tired." he grabbed the water that someone had moved off the fire and started filling the waterskins. Once it was all poured away he shook his head then stood up.

"I'm going to get more water, I'll be right back." he said as he started walking in the direction of the river.

*   *   *

Kinley followed the river for a while, not wanting to return. He found a petrified log and sat down, the sealed leather bag already filled with water and tied to his waist. His mind was cycling through questions but now a few of them were *Why did I stare at her arm like that? Was it really glowing or was I just imagining it? I know I heard her voice when she was talking to me, but why didn't I care?* His confusion was unsettling to him. He wondered why The Crystal Heart didn't come in and clear it up, answering what he desired to know. He still found himself unsure of being the one that could actually collect and re-assemble all the shards of The Crystal Heart.

"I am so sorry my love," he said out loud, "That your heart was shattered, I can't imagine how painful it must be to feel one part of yourself separated in every direction every moment, all the time."

There was no answer, but he didn't expect one. He looked into the waters before him, nothing could be seen in the darkness, he wanted to reach his hand in and feel the coolness against his skin, but now he felt a constant lingering fear of the strange acid green fish whenever he was near the water. "I guess I sort of understand my heart now feels separated from you, if not for the shards in my pocket I don't think I would allow myself to live." he said to himself this time.

"Well, that's a little melodramatic." said a voice

behind him. He recognized the tone in Arissa's voice instantly.

"What are you doing here?" he asked her, feeling that she intruded into his private time.

Kinley saw the look on her face change from a lighthearted joking expression to a pained one. He judged that she had read the tone in his voice. "Sorry." he said curtly offering no further explanation.

"It's Okay," she said, her expression changing again to the light hearted one, this time it was accompanied by a smirk, "I was just coming to make sure that you weren't lying unconscious. I guess I could have left when I heard you talking, but then I just wanted to tell you that if you ever needed to talk to me, well, that I was here for you. What you are going through isn't exactly normal after all."

Now it was Kinley's turn to look hurt, not at her words, but at realizing that she was right. When he was in the memories of The Crystal Heart, everything felt so natural and normal to him. Now that he was here, he felt like an outsider to everyone else. His life had completely changed and he had an immense responsibility on his shoulders, one that would change the path of Arathia and all the other places on the planet.

"I just wish I could speak to him here, like I did there." he said looking at where he assumed his feet were.

Arissa's face softened to a sympathetic frown, and her brows furrowed. "Kinley I cannot imagine what you are going through, no one can actually. You are special, you are different and I have known that forever, but I didn't know how. I know that there are a lot of confusing things going on and probably a lot of questions running through your mind, but I guess you'll just have to figure them out without his help. Either he doesn't know the answer or you'll have to learn something else to learn the answer to the questions that... you... are asking... yourself... I think I just confused myself." she attempted to make him laugh and a weak chuckle passed his lips.

"I understand what you're getting at," he said, "but I still wish I were back there, in his memories." Kinley closed his eyes, remembering whatever details he could. The creatures that were running, swimming, hopping or flying about in every direction. Remembering the moss and the trees, but the clearest thing that he remembered were the waters. He remembered from his own memory, not from his imagination and the stories that his mother had told him.

"You know," he said, "Ma and Keeva didn't do the waters justice in their stories. I mean, yes, they did look like a sea of diamonds, but they forgot to mention the rainbows that danced along the surface and the fish jumping out of the warm water joyously. They forgot about the brightly colored birds flying overhead and the plants that floated amongst the diamonds on the water. If only for the reason of the waters, I am glad that I am going to restore The Crystal Heart."

"I think I'm just going to go ahead and leave you here to think a while, if the water bag is full I'll go ahead and bring that back with me, it looks like you have enough there to finish filling the water skins." She told him.

"Yeah, thanks." he said as he lifted the large sealed pouch from the ground filled water and handed it to her. "Do you think this water has to last us until the Trading Post?" he asked.

"Probably," she replied, "I know the only reason that we've stopped for this long was basically for me to train, that's finished. The burning is finished and there is a lot of extra fish left for the walk, I think Fallyn will probably wait for people to have one more sleep and then while they are fresh from that we'll head towards the Trading Post."

"Okay, I'll see you back at Keeva's." he said leaving his head lowered towards the ground. She walked off carrying the water and full satisfaction in knowing that, as of that moment, she wasn't going to have to stab Kinley through the heart again.

She paused and turned, "Please don't get bit again." she said smiling slyly.

Kinley sat for a while, allowing his mind to wander until he was relaxed enough to head back to the camp where there was still water boiling. All the waterskins were full so he assumed that this water was for washing up. He stripped down and used his hands to rub some of the dirt off his body, then scooped up some of the water and rinsed his body. The whole time doing so, he didn't take his eyes off the back pocket of his pants.

He slid back into his dirty garments, noticing the textural difference between his skin and the rough filthy clothing that was scraping against it. He sat by the fire listening to the sound of Keeva and his mother lightly snoring in the tent. Eventually he drifted to sleep, the glow of the flame died down and the intensity of the heat faded with it.

* * *

When Kinley woke up, Keeva already had the camp packed away. The fire was built back up, but to a smaller caliber. He sat up and noticed three people around the fire. Enat, Keeva and Fallyn were chatting, sipping from a waterskin, steam rose from the openings so Kinley was sure that it wasn't just water.

"Glad to see that you're doing better Kinley, we're about to start walking and we were just discussing where you would be in the procession." Fallyn said.

"Where I will be?" he asked still drowsy and not fully grasping the words that were being spoken to him. He yawned when he started to speak again, "I'll be in the back with the rest of the fighters."

"Well, that's the thing, you're no longer sick, but with your physical changes, the council isn't convinced that you're completely healed. They're saying that you could be a hazard. The Ree-Kyae have already attacked and I don't think they will try again for a while, but if you start lagging behind and get lost, well... we don't want to accidentally leave you behind. I was thinking that, if you wouldn't mind, we could use your help pulling the carts."

Kinley rubbed the sleep from his eyes and stretched his arms out over his head. "I guess that would work." he said as he brought his arms back to his sides. He stood up and tied a waterskin to his waste so he'd have something to drink as he walked. "Alright, let's go."

"Sure are eager to get pulling, aren't you?" Keeva said smiling at him.

Kinley said nothing, instead he yawned as he moved to sit. His clothes were filthy from sleeping on the dirt, and dried mud clung to his skin from washing up before bed. He visited with the three people he had woken up to, eventually Fallyn excused himself and made his way to the council.

Fallyn had called everyone for the typical before-the-walk pep talk; the layout of it had changed. Fallyn was at the front and behind him, in two rows, were the council members.

"We'd like to welcome Kinley back, first of all. We expect that, since the Ree-Kyae have already attacked us, they won't be back. It should be a straight shot to the Trading Post, however we will still have the fighters posted at the back and we will still be walking in defense formation, just in case. There should be enough food and water to continue walking straight on."

Kinley looked around to try to find Arissa, she was standing with the rest of the fighters in full armor, the fires around the camp allowed him to see her relatively well as they glimmered and shined off her armor and those around her.

The council and Fallyn had broken up and each family, already packed up, had gone to extinguish their fires before falling into the defense formation that they had walked in since the news of the Ree-Kyae threat. A feeling had crept into Kinleys core and it had been pestering him since he woke from death. It was the feeling that what he was doing, at this moment, would be the last time. No other explanation, just that everything he was doing, for instance sleeping on the ground in front of the fire while Keeva and Enat slept in the tent near him, would be the last time that he would do so. It was unsettling to think that, as this feeling suggested, this would be the last time that he set out to a destination with the family and friends he had known his entire life.

He looked around, paying close attention to the faces of the people around him; he studied each face until he came across his mothers and felt instantly sad. He walked over to her "Ma, looks like this is the last stop before the Trading Post."

She smiled at him "I know sweetie, when we get there I need to talk to you about something important."

"Oh, why can't you just tell me now?" he asked, noticing her eyes dart back and forth.

"I don't have time to give you what I need to." she said as she shuffled away to where all of the woman were meeting, leaving no reasoning as to what she stated.

Kinley felt that he had no choice but to drop the subject as he made his way toward the carts. Once everyone was ready to go, he grabbed the pole on the end of one of the carts and hoisted it up until it was resting on his shoulder. He looked to the pole on his other side waiting for someone to come grab it and help him pull but no one seemed to be willing to help. He looked around in the darkness and couldn't see anyone coming to his aide.

He walked to the back of the cart and pulled a leather strap from it, which he tied to the ends of both of the poles. He grabbed the center of it and pulled, the cart inched forward, picking up pace as it moved. Kinley wasn't sure when the cart gathered enough momentum and he found that all he had to do was steer it, occasionally the cart would bump a rock and attempt to tip over, when that happened he quickly grabbed the poles at the front and steadied it.

After a while his hands and shoulders started to ache from the constant steadying of the cart and all that he could think of was how painful it would be if he had to completely pull the cart himself as well. Excited chattering broke out between some of the people pulling the carts and it seemed to move back throughout the group. He listened intently to see if he could hear what was going on and managed to catch a few words, two of which being "Almost there."

Chapter Eight

The Trading Post

It came into view slowly, and before they knew it, they were at the bridge waiting to cross into the Trading Post. The guards there were heavily armed, both ranged and melee weapons hung from their backs and around their waists. Kinley watched as Fallyn walked to one of the guards, Kinley guessed that this was the guard in charge due to the difference in uniform between him and other. Fallyn and the guard shared words privately, then the guard stepped away and waved them in. Kinley looked around; the Trading Post looked even bigger than it did the last time he was there.

He could only see a little bit of it, until he and his tribe walked in anyway. Right now he could make out the large structures formed from chunks of stone, which made up the guest cabins. When members of the nomadic tribes came to the Trading Post they stayed in these until they were ready to go again. He knew that past those were the stands the vendors set up, the nomadic tribes came and traded their findings with the vendors as well as other tribes that had made their way to the Trading Post.

In the very center of the Trading Post was a large rough wooden pole sticking from the ground and reaching high into the sky. When The Crystal Heart was suspended on the mountain the wooden pole was the largest tree in Arathia, and its leaves spread to cover almost the entire Trading Post. In the time since no one had bothered to cut it completely down, in hopes that it might start growing again. Occasionally, when there was a need for wood, the council members would meet and decide if the need was great enough to take from the pole. Then one of them would strip away a few large pieces and they would be fashioned into firewood or tent poles among other things.

Fallyn started walking forward, and as he did the guards parted, and bowed in respect and welcome. The tired nomadic tribe followed Fallyn to one of the stone building; the bottom was one open hollow room with support columns, which went from floor to ceiling. It was completely open on one side, and on the far side stone stairs led to a hole in the ceiling, or floor, depending which level you were on. It took a little while for all the carts to make their way into the open room and even longer for each family to unpack their belongings. There were a few different floors, and around ten rooms on each floor, enough rooms in the building for each family to have one, and there still be rooms left over. Fallyn and the council stayed on floor closest to the ground, everyone picked his or her own rooms from there.

There was no reason to unpack the tents, but the dried moss mattresses were rolled out onto the stone floor in every room of the building. Small fires were built as far away from the mattress as possible, to keep warm. Kinley and Enat decided that it would be less lonely if Keeva stayed with them. The mattresses touched as they were spread in a "U" shape, fire in against the stone wall. Exhausted from their walk, Kinley decided to lay down and attempt to sleep. He closed his eyes and laid there, not noticing when he actually lost consciousness of the real world.

*   *   *

Kinley opened his eyes after giving up on sleeping, he was in the stone building, in the Trading Post, but it was bright again. He stared up at the stone ceiling above him, and felt the cold stone below him. It took his brain a moment to come to the realization that his moss mattress wasn't under him. This time there was no waiting for his eyes to adjust to the brightness around him. Kinley stood up and noticed that, not only were there no mattresses on the stone floor but there were no people in the room with him, there were no remains of the fire that was blazing and when Kinley stood silently, listening, no echoes of voices came from the other rooms. He was completely alone. The comforting presence of the Crystal Heart wasn't even there with him. A tear fell from Kinley's eye; he felt it slide down his cheek and across his lips to his chin.

One tear was all that fell and when he felt it

drip from his chin, he looked down in time to see it sparkle and splash on the ground. The drip started bubbling and expanding, pulling itself outward from the middle in waves. It grew wider and wider and as it did it grew taller. Eventually Kinley's tear had grown to his height and taken on the basic shape of a person. As Kinley watched, detail started to form from the top of the head and spread downward. The hair was the first thing that changed. A liquid shape took place a top the head and spread out shoulder length, the hair was cropped short. A ripple spread across the face, and as it did facial featured emerged. Kinley was able to tell that the figure before him was female. The shape took on color and became opaque; before he knew it, Arissa was armor-clad and shining in the light of The Crystal Heart.

She smiled at him, revealing her white teeth. "Are you ready?" She asked.

Kinley was pleased that she was there with him, he didn't like being alone. "Ready?" he was unclear on what she was asking him.

"Yes, Ready, to go…" she asked.

"Where are we going?" He asked her, but instead of answering with words, she shifted her gaze to the Mountains of The Crystal Heart.

Arissa's form shimmered, the color and opacity left quickly and the tear started changing, it grew a little taller than Kinley and had more of a muscular build. Once the shape was right, detail started to spread again, using the same ripple like movement that had brought Arissa's face into existence. Before he could put together who was standing in front of him, the voice started speaking.

"Listen, I know we aren't friends," it said as

color spread down the figure from head to toe, the face of the person still hadn't solidified but Kinley could tell who it was from the voice. "but I'm going too." Peadar was fully formed from the tear, standing in front of Kinley with a stern and stubborn look on his face.

"You don't even know where we're going." Kinley told him.

"Neither do you." He replied, his face softened a little and he looked to his feet. "Arissa has to go with you, and if she's going, then I am too."

"But you don't even know what we're going to do, for all you know we could be swimming with the monsters in the river, could even be walking over Perseverance Pass to spit in the eye of the Ree-Kyae king."

"It doesn't matter where we go, or what we are going to do, if Arissa is with you, you can bet that I will be standing right there with her. Now, are you ready to go?"

Kinley was about to answer when he started shimmering and fading, just as Arissa had. The tear had returned to its blank canvas state. The body had shrunk down and turned more feminine, detail popped again, this time it started from the arm of the being, and rippled from that point. "Ma?" he asked, "Is that you?"

"Remember, there is something I need to talk to you about, don't leave before then."

"Arissa, and Peadar, fine, but you are not going with me." he said putting his foot down and ending with finality.

Enat let out a laugh. "I am too damn old to be going with you; I can't do what you're going to have to do. I just wanted to make sure that you remembered to talk to me, I have to give you something." She moved her hand over to her arm, the spot where Kinley had seen the light coming from before. Kinley thought that she was going to rub it, as she normally does when stressed or uncomfortable. Instead, her fingers passed through her skin and a ripple spread up and down her arm. She pulled her hand out and, as she did, something came with it. Between her thumb and forefinger was a liquid silver shard, just like the two that he kept with him, only smaller.

She went to place the shard in his hand, but as her hand moved closer to him her form wavered and the color fled from the shard. Kinley watched the grey retreat into her hand, darkening her already tanned skin a little more. She dropped the shard, which had started to glow with its strange pulsating light, and as it fell into his hands, it lost its solid form. It splashed through his fingers leaving a wet stain on his hands, and the stone floor below them. He looked into his mother's eyes, she smiled and her solid shape melted away and splashed to the ground.

The puddle started to boil in on itself again, this time pulling inward until nothing but the single tearstain was left. He watched it on the cold stone until it had dried up, leaving nothing behind. He felt warmth on his back and turned, the stone wall that was behind him had disappeared leaving an exposed view of The Mountains of The Crystal Heart. The light on top was growing brighter with each pulse that it put out; eventually Kinley had to look away from the light. Feeling something inside pull him, he took a step towards the light, bumping into the cutout in the stone wall.

Still feeling that pull, he walked toward the opening of the room and through it, into the vast darkness of the hallway. He found it strange that even though he was in the world of The Crystal Heart, and he felt the warmth of the light on his skin, that this strange cold darkness still existed. He made his way down the flights of stone stairs until he was in the open room at the base of the building. He stared at the light of The Crystal Heart.

It took him what felt like forever to reach The Mountains of The Crystal Heart, like his whole journey down the strength river to the Trading Post. He thought about that as he walked, thought about how pointless it was to follow a river just to get to the Trading Post and pick another river to follow. An endless journey of the same monotonous task, searching out dried foliage and pieces of cloth to sustain everyday life. Kinley remembered as he walked, when he was younger, his first viable memory of the Ree-Kyae. Kinley only remembered the face, looking down at him, scarred and melted flesh with sores oozing clear liquid. He remembered the slits where the nose would be on its face, he remembered the teeth all pointed as if every single one of them were canines.

Most of all he remembered the glowing skin and the growling sound that it made deep in its throat as something heavy and large smashed against the side of its head. In memory, Kinley felt the warm blood on his face and the stench of the rotting Ree-Kyae flesh fill his nose to the point where he wrenched himself away from his memories and looked around, half expecting to see a flash of white darting around in the shadows. Nothing was there, however the rotting stench of flesh lingered in his nose. After pausing for a moment he started walking again, picking up the pace as he made his way to where The Crystal Heart rested.

Step after step, he felt the springy moss under his bare feet and as he got closer to the mountains he could feel the moss get patchy and give way to dirt, then rock. As he moved closer the pull that he felt inside him didn't weaken, but instead, grew stronger and more intense. Kinley stopped to catch his breath and noticed that his feet were now resting at a slight vertical incline. Kinley looked up and realized that he was at the Mountains of The Crystal Heart; the pull was more physical now. He felt a tug in his chest and his body recoiled in surprise.

Kinleys feet were sore from the long walk and now he had to climb it, he looked high up to the top and, for the first time, he realized how incredibly tall the mountain was. *When the legend said the highest point in Arathia, tit certainly wasn't kidding.* He thought to himself.

There was no pathway to where The Crystal Heart sat, so Kinley started out climbing the gigantic mountain on his own. He hoped that he would find a place where he could rest. Hand over hand and foot over foot, Kinley started making his way up the mountain, occasionally slipping. Right after he started climbing, he found a small ledge, just wide enough for him to lay down safely. Kinley closed his eyes and saw a dull green color through his eyelids. He buried his face in his in the crease of his arm and fell asleep. Before dozing off Kinley felt a little worried, he didn't know if he is was going to go to sleep and wake up in the darkness or if he would dream.

Neither happened, he stayed there, asleep yet still completely aware of his surroundings. He could see every little critter that scuttled around him, his eyes were closed, but somehow he saw it happening in his brain. Time passed slowly as he slept, and he was aware of how much time he was spending sleeping, however he also remembered that time passed a lot slower in the memories of The Crystal Heart than in his real world.

Kinley felt the soreness and stiffness in his limbs dissipate so he opened his eyes and continued his climb up the mountain. Kinleys recently bestowed strength helped him, as he made his way up higher and higher his speed increased. It still took a while but he found himself at the mountains summit a lot sooner than a normal person would have. Kinley walked towards The Crystal Heart with his arm outstretched, but as his hand was about to make contact with it, he felt a pull in his chest, strangely enough this one lead to nowhere.

He felt his arm pull back involuntarily followed by a pain in his chest where the new pull originated. Kinley pushed his arm forward but he felt that The Crystal Heart was repelling his touch. Kinley wasn't going to give up, he still pushed through, the closer his hand came to touching the smooth surface the sharper the pain in his chest was. Kinley felt a hand on each shoulder and two hands on the arm that he was pushing toward The Crystal Heart. Those two hands pushed with all the force they could muster and he felt the smooth surface on his skin. The pain instantly left his chest, he turned to look whom the people were and found Arissa and Peadar standing behind him. They smiled at him and spoke in a singular calming voice "You can't do it alone."

* * *

Kinley's eyes shot open, there were burning embers sitting in the pit where the fire used to be. Everyone had long since gone to sleep; Kinley rubbed his eyes as he sat up. he looked around, Enat was still asleep on one of the dried moss mattresses, but Keeva's was empty, Kinley assumed that she was out wandering the Trading Post.

"Ma," he said sleepily. "Wake up." he crawled over to her on his hands and knees, grabbing and gently shaking her arm.

"Wha... Kinley, what's going on?" she said alarmed, it wasn't like him to wake her up.

"Ma," he said calmly, "you wanted to talk to me."

"Huh? Yeah, I did. You really didn't have to wake me up though."

"Yes, I did, I have to go Ma, before the next sleep. Arissa and Peadar are going with me, but they don't know it yet."

"Then I suppose I should give you want I need to..." she sat up and rubbed her eyes, then looked down at her forearm. "It's going to be strange, not having this with me anymore; it's been there for so long I can barely imagine life without it."

Enat reached down pinching the skin of her forearm pulling upward., "Get a blade Kinley," she said to him, "and cut me right here."

Kinley reached for a blade, but felt his hand moving on its own as it changed direction, he reached into his back pocket and grabbed the leather pouch holding the two shards of The Crystal Heart. He unwrapped it, pulling his original shard out. He put up his own silent protest as his hand brought the shard to his mother's golden skin. As it got closer, the spot below the pinched skin started glowing with the same light of The Crystal Heart. The vibrating shard in Kinleys hand was glowing and the vibrating intensified as his hand pressed the sharp tip of the shard across his mother's skin. A red line instantly appeared and Enat wigged the fingers that pinched her skin back and forth, working something out from within.

Eventually Kinley saw the point of a grey rock coming from the gash in Enats forearm. For the first time, Kinley looked up at his mother's face; he saw pain in the expression that occupied it. More of the shard that had been embedded in Kinley's mothers arm exposed itself as it moved, slowly out of her forearm. Kinley reached for the shard, wanting to pull it out of his mother's arm, but his hand stopped and hovered over it, not moving no matter how much Kinley willed it to. Kinley watched Enats eyes as his hand stood still over the shard that protruded from his mother's forearm. It seemed to him that with each twist of her fingers Enat put herself through even more pain. Kinley regained control of his arm and reached down towards the shard without thinking he wrapped his fingers around the long and thin piece and pulled it free.

Once the shard left his mother's arm the wound healed leaving nothing but a thin red line of wet blood, she brought her finger over it and wiped it away bringing an undisturbed patch of skin into view.

"There," she said to him, "you needed that." Kinley looked down at the new shard, and though it had been inside of his mother for so long, it looked brand new and polished. "You know it's strange, but feeling the way that it thumped inside my arm grew to be second heartbeat, and without it, I don't feel the same."

"I know exactly what you mean." Kinley wrapped the three shards back in leather and returned them to his pocket thankful for the constant feeling of security. "Without them I would be... uneasy." He allowed his hand to grace his back pocket before placing it in his mothers. "I know that you're going to miss me, and I am going to miss you too Ma, but you know I have to go right?"

"Yes, and it won't take long, I hope."

"I want you know, that when the light returns, I'll be on my way back to you, hold that in your heart while I am gone."

"You've changed so much," she said as she grabbed his neck and pulled him into a hug, "but you are still the man that I raised you to be, no matter what you look like."

A tear slid down Enats cheek as she held Kinley, "I am so proud of you." she used the hand closest to the tear to wipe it away. "I have made my share of mistakes and failures as a mother, but it seems that no matter the job I have done, you have more than surpassed any hopes that I could have had for you."

Kinley looked at her face and noticed that her eyes were swollen with pent up tears. "I'll be back Ma, and when I do return, you and I are going into the rivers for a swim."

Enat smiled and released Kinley from her grip "Go, find Arissa and Peadar, I hope you find a way for me to hear from you while you are away. I'll tell Fallyn you've gone, but not where."

"I love you Ma."

"I love you too Kinley."

With that, Kinley turned and walked out the rectangular hole in the wall and into the hallway that led to the stone staircase. He followed it until he was out of the building. The full extent of the Trading Post shocked him every time he saw it up close. The horizon was dotted with firelight as far as he could see, and at each one, he knew there was someone looking to trade what they had gathered or made on their journeys around Arathia. At first, he meandered around looking for Peadar and Arissa while seeing what the venders had to offer. There was no one vender that specialized in one certain thing, but at each roughly constructed booth was a multitude of different items.

Having walked with his small group for so long, Kinley was not used to the noise of the Trading Post. His ears seemed to be constantly affronted with a cacophony of hoots and wailings from the people around him. The bustling jumble of face after face in the crowd assaulted his eyes and left him disoriented and confused. He stopped to rest, leaning his body weight onto his arm, which he set down on one of the merchant booths.

He closed his eyes but, instead of helping, this just exacerbated the situation. The voices of the people around him seemed to be booming in his head; meaningless conversations about fish bone combs inlaid with shiny rocks and colorfully dyed and abrasive tent fabrics seemed to take precedence over his own thoughts. He tried to focus his attention on any one conversation at a time, but his mind jumped around to bits and pieces of different ones. "I found this fish bone comb... tangled up in the sleeves of a dead... mother gave it to me right after I got... hit directly in the face by... the first female fighter..."

So the rumors are spreading, Kinley thought, *that gives me more of a reason to hurry. If the tribe itself was as divided as it was, who knows how much protest Fallyn and the others will see in a place as large as the Trading Post once they are confirmed.*

Struggling to gain control of this thought, Kinley pushed the other conversations from his focus; before he realized what he was doing his hand was in his back pocket. He brought one of the three shards out and held it firmly in his fist. Blood seeped through his closed fingers and dripped to the ground, immediately being soaked in upon contact.

"Hey, are you alright?" The person renting the booth noticed the blood dripping and the pained look on Kinley's face.

"Yes, I am looking for someone and it can be... overwhelming with so many here is all."

"No meeting plan, huh? That can definitely be a problem."

"They don't know that I am looking, not yet anyway."

Kinley pushed off the merchants' booth and pulled his arm back to his body, no longer forcing it to support him. His senses seemed to dull as he took each step, blood still dripped from his hand, and eventually he regained focus. He continued walking and searching for Arissa and Peadar, while doing so he kept an ear out for any whispered hints or clues as to where they might be found. He continued between the rows of crudely constructed booths noticing the knickknacks and supplies that were sitting out. He kept an ear out for more whispered rumors about the female fighter, and found he didn't have to listen to hard.

It seemed to Kinley that just about every person in the Trading Post had heard about Arissa, he noticed a brief glint of firelight out of the corner of his eye, and realized why. Arissa was standing, in full armor, next to the fire with an angry expression painted across her face. Behind her, Kinley noticed Peadar muscles tensed. In front of them, two men stood, both tall, both burley, and both with angry expressions. Before Kinley was able to move Arissa had leapt at one of the men, she swung her body around his side and wrapped her metal and leather clad legs around his neck, she swung her full body weight down and pulled the man's top half with her. His feet flew out from under him and his head smacked the packed earth with a sickening sound.

Peadar looked like he was ready to jump in and knock their heads together; leaving them bleeding and unconscious, but he did nothing. Arissa untangled her legs from around the strangers' neck and swept them under the other man's leg, knocking him down in one swift movement. The first person stood up blood was dripping down his face from his forehead. Arissa was up in a flash, her teeth were barred and there was an animalistic look in her eyes. She whipped around and thrust her heel into his gut, full force. The second man was getting up and Arissa turned on her heel, and brought her other one down on his stomach leaving him gasping in pain.

Kinley looked to Peadar and noticed his smug expression, which began with a pair of steely eyes and ended in a twisted smile. He grabbed Arissa, who was still kicking the men on the ground in a fury, and pulled her away, a fire still burned in her eyes. When they were walking past, Kinley followed keeping pace, he knew better than to try to talk Arissa out of a rage. Apparently, Peadar did to because they walked in silence, and Kinley noticed that the further away from the crowd they got, the more relaxed his grip became.

They reached the stone building where his group was staying, and entered into the bottom floor, the one with no walls. Empty carts were parked everywhere, occasionally one would have something in it. The carts that functioned as buildings, such as Esras' medical cart, were collapsed and the contents were taken up the stone steps to empty quarters which functioned as storage. Kinley watched as Arissa and Peadar weaved their way in between carts until they reached the stone steps. He called to them before they took their first steps.

"Hey, hold on." they looked around and saw Kinley coming from the back. Before he thought about what he was saying, he blurted out "We have to leave." Peadar looked at Arissa with confusion in his eyes, which was lacking from her own gaze. Kinley caught up to them and, this time, thought about what he was going to say next. 'We have to find the rest of the shards," he spoke under his breath, "and then I have to reunite it."

Peadar watched them both; he noticed the look of understanding on Arissa's face and the look of excitement on Kinleys. He searched his own face to try and figure out what expression he wore, it seemed to be shifting to different ones before he could grasp the meaning of what was currently there. "Listen," Kinley said to Peadar, "I know I'm going, and Arissa knows that she is coming with me, and we both know that you are going anywhere she is. So, instead of sitting here and explaining everything you both should go upstairs, get a few of your belongings, say goodbye to those you love and meet me back down here as quickly as possible."

Arissa nodded her head once in a swift motion and grabbed Peadars arm, pulling him up the stone steps after her. As they made their way up the steps, Peadar tried to fish for answers to a few of the multitude of questions that were swimming around in his head. Arissa drug him into where she was staying, and he stood as he watched her toss a few belongings into a roughly constructed fiber bag that looked like it had a very course texture.

"Are you going to tell me what the hell is going on yet." he said to her as she grabbed his arm and pulled him down the hallway and up the steps to where he and his grandfather were staying.

"There is no time now, we have to get you ready and out of here." she half spoke and half screamed at him.

"But what am I going to tell my grandfather?" he asked.

"Whatever it is that your grandfather needs to know, he will already. I am sure that The Crystal Heart let him know you were going to be leaving."

"The Crystal Heart," He exclaimed questioningly, "What does that have to do with anything?"

"I told you, there is no time now, just get your stuff together and let's get out of here. Your grandfather has a much different store to create now."

Caedmon was waiting for them at the entrance to the room a smile was plastered on his face but his eyes were filled with worry. "There are a lot of questions going through my mind at this moment, however there is no time. I've already packed all your stuff away, just come here and give me a hug." Caedmon hobbled over to Peadar and wrapped his arms around him, pulling him into a forceful embrace. Before releasing Peadar Caedmon whispered into his ear "I'm so proud of you, and your parents would be to."

Caedmon let go of Peadar with a push and turned towards the fire in an attempt to hide the tears that were now rolling down his cheek.

"Your bag is in the corner, everything you could possibly need is in it. I hope your task is completed quickly and you return to me unharmed." Caedmon waved his hand in in the general direction of the bag. Peadar looks from the bag to his grandfather and back again, then picked the bag up off the stone ground. "There is one other thing I have to ask of you before you leave." Caedmon said, his voice wavering, "can you keep a detailed memory of the events that happen, this is your journey and its one that everyone will want to know, it's one that is worthy of a massive illumistration."

Now Peadar knew that whatever he, Kinley and Arissa were up to was going to change history. Illumistrations weren't something that just anyone could see, and massive illumistrations were only done on very rare occasions. Peadar slung the roughly constructed bag over his shoulder and turned towards the stone archway and saw Arissa now standing there waiting for him, still armor clad but now with a course bag slung over her own shoulder, she must have gone to collect her own stuff while he was talking to his grandfather. She had a look on her face that showed complete concentration and one in her eyes that said she was ready for anything, which didn't surprise him.

She impatiently stood, tapping the heavy toe of her thick boot to the stone floor while she waited for the two of them to finish talking.

"Goodbye gramps." Peadar said as he walked past Arissa, his hand grabbed at hers and rubbed gently as they both started down the stone steps.

*   *   *

Kinley watched the stairs intently while he waited for Arissa and Peadar. He had put together a bag of his possessions while Arissa and Peadar were upstairs getting their stuff. His mother wasn't in the room; he assumed that she was now out roaming the Trading Post. Keeva waved to him as he started down the stairs but he didn't notice, instead his mind was racing through various scenarios of what could happen while they were out on their own. He questioned if the tribe would notice their absence or be handicapped by three of the best fighters leaving on their own journey.

Arissa and Peadar came bounding down the stairs two steps at a time, their feet fell in perfect unison, leaving barely an echo in the empty stairwell. There was silence between them and Kinley tried to imagine what was going on in their own heads, he wondered if The Crystal Heart had told Peadar anything about the journey in his dreams and wondered if Arissa had told him anything while they were away. Kinley was sure that Arissa already knew where they were going, as she had been in possession of a shard of The Crystal Heart her link to it was very strong, he could imagine her mentally preparing to leave her family and friends.

One thing that he knew for sure was that she was running through the recent events in her mind, his change of features, the timing of herself becoming the first female fighter, her fondness of Peadar. And he knew that she found herself wondering if everything that had taken place was spontaneity, some kind of divine plan, or destiny.

Before Kinley had a chance to contemplate any further Peadar and Arissa were standing in front of him. Neither was sweating, nor out of breath, which surprised Kinley considering that they both ran up and down as many stairs as they had. They walked to the entrance and exit stations where the guards were posted and found Caedmon and Fallyn standing there waiting.

"Those three, right there." Fallyn said pointing in their direction.

"Either we have complete permission to leave, or we are being stopped before we even start." Arissa whispered to the other two.

"I don't think we're being stopped, gramps was pretty happy with whatever we are doing, look at the expression on his face. Do you think he would still be smiling if we were being stopped?" Arissa and Kinley both shook their heads in agreement with Peadar. They slowed their speed as they approached Caedmon Fallyn and the two guards, stopping in front of them.

"Let them through." Fallyn said as the guards looked apprehensively back and forth.

"We already told you," said one of them, "we

can't let out a group with this small a number of people out of the Trading Post. It's suicide."

"Well, add the two of us in." Said Caedmon, apparently losing his patience for the run around that the guards were giving them. "I am Caedmon, the foremost storyteller and illumistrator in all of Arathia. Fallyn is a tribe leader, you cannot deny the orders that we give you, no matter how obscene you feel they are, in fact, right now I am ordering you to lick the bottom of your own boot." he said to the guard who had denied allowing the group of three out of the Trading Post.

"My Boot?" said the guard, looking quizzically at Caedmon, "Are you serious?"

"Well I wasn't before, I was going to stop you before you started, however with the disrespect of actually questioning me I'm going to go ahead and let you do it. Now call your commander over." Caedmon said with embers starting to glow in his eyes.

Fallyn looked at the guard and then to Caedmon, wondering if he was actually going to make this guard lick his own boot. The disrespectful guard moved to go get his commander but Caedmon stopped him in his tracks with his staff, slamming it hard into his shins.

"Not you," he said to the disrespectful guard, "Him" he pointed to the other guard. "I don't want you running off before you are able to taste what you've been stepping in."

As they waited for the commander to show, Caedmon's eyes never left the disrespectful guards face. When the commander and the other guard returned to settle the scuffle, irritation showed on the commanders' face.

"Alrigh' what da issue 'ere be?" he asked gruffly, Caedmon instantly rolled his eyes at the dialect the man spoke. "You travel the Endurance River?" he asked him.

"Yeh, ow'd yuh know?" the commander asked.

"Well," said Caedmon, "You're nose has been broken, same with your arm and you walk with a limp. The Endurance trail has done similar things to many that travel alongside the river."

"Yeh," said the commander, "yuh walk wif uh limp 'urself."

"Yes, however I don't have the same accent you do." it was plain to the commander that Caedmon was already irritated by the disrespectful soldier so he decided not to pursue the shortness of Caedmon's tone. "Well, 'neway, what 'ur issue be?"

"Your guard is refusing to follow the orders of Caedmon and me, and as I am sure you know, as the most well-known of the storytellers your guards should follow whatever he says or it may come back on you. In addition, I am a tribe leader; my word is law among your guards. I suggest you have them follow all of Caedmon's orders before I meet with the Trading Post grand counsel or before Caedmon decides to tell a story of this day." Fallyn said sneaking a smile at Caedmon.

"Hmmm," said the guard, mulling over Fallyn's words, thinking hard before answering. "Yeh, 'course 'ur righ'. Da guar' was wron' un not listnin' tuh yuh." he turned to the disrespectful guard, "I wan' yuh ta do what'ver da storytella' say fo' ya tuh do, an' yuh will ha' some punnishmen' fo' yuhr disrespec'fullness."

"But," started the guard with a pleading look in his eyes, "I have to do absolutely everything?"

The commander had an angry look in his own eyes now, "Eh, I will not 'ave my own men disrespec'in me, when yuhr finish wif what da ol' man 'as uh yeh, yuh'll be reportin' tuh me." and with that the commander walked away.

"And now," Caedmon said, "as your commander said, I believe it's time for you to follow the "old mans" orders and lick your boot and after that you'll be allowing these three out of the Trading Post, with no sideways glances or disrespect." The guard sat down and started to pull his boot to his face, however this was not what Caedmon had in mind. "Now, as a guard, the first thing that you should know is you are never to sit unless instructed you, you will stand as you lick your boot." Anger flashed in the guards' eyes for a brief second as he stood up. He pulled his boot to his face while balancing on one leg and toppled over onto his side.

Caedmon chuckled, "That's enough, no need to go any further. You've had enough punishment and embarrassment from me, your commander still has more in store for you, just let my grandson and his two companions through." Kinley noticed some sniggering coming from all around, he assumed it was from the other guards that were posted around the area. The disrespectful guard picked himself up off the ground for the second time and waved Kinley, Arissa, and Peadar over the bridge, escorting them to the end of it, and then walking out of sight in the darkness.

The lonely feeling that Kinley had felt before was returning as he stood in the darkness. He turned to look back at the Trading Post and saw fire after fire pressing high into the darkness, disappearing from view about half way up was the building his nomadic tribe was staying in. "Right now this seems like an impossible task." he stated to Arissa and Peadar. Arissa nodded in the darkness, and Peadar responded under his breathe with "If I knew what this *task* was, I might agree."

Kinley sighed and turned to him. "May The Crystal Heart damn you Peadar, can't you wait for anything? We are going off to face perilous danger in order to find the remaining shards of The Crystal Heart and we are going to reassemble it, then I am going to have to perform some mysterious ritual in order to make it whole again." Peadar's mouth hung wide open and he turned to face Arissa. "Is he serious?" he asked her.

She smiled at him at him. "It sure is a good thing that you insisted on coming with us."

"I insisted?" he asked.

"Oh yes," she said, "don't you remember?" she pulled her face up to his and kissed him on the cheek.

"Remember... what?" he asked, pretending to forget what they were saying.

"Good, now let's get going," she said to them, "which direction to we go again Kinley?"

He looked around in the dark, and turned in a circle. Unsure he said, "I don't exactly know…"

To Be Continued…

ABOUT THE AUTHOR

Anthony M. Swinsinski started working for an independently owned publishing company at the age of thirteen years old. He started out in production, and then moved onto layout and inputting changes. His writing started with Internet reference guides, after that he moved onto bartending. He returned to writing with a bartending guide titled *Mixology: How to Make 27 Drinks Perfectly and Be Your Own Bartender*. While Bartending, Anthony started developing the concept for *The Crystal Heart* trilogy, and has been working on that ever since.

The Crystal Heart: Journey

An Excerpt

Chapter One

Heading Out

Arissa watched Kinley with a questioning look in her eyes that made him uncomfortable. He switched to look at Peadar, who had the same curious look in his eyes. "Well…" said Arissa letting her single word fade away. "Well, what?" asked Kinley.

"Well," she replied, "which way do we go now?" Peadar nodded in agreement.

"Uhhh…" said Kinley, now letting his word fade to nothingness. His eyes scanned the darkness for some sort of sign. "I don't… really… know."

"Wait, you mean that you are dragging us out here, away from the safety of the tribe, of the Trading Post of all things, and you don't even know where the hell we are going?"

"Not exactly where we are going, no, but don't

worry," he said, "it'll come to me, somehow."

Arissa seemed to relax a little in the shoulders. "It seems that these things do always work out in his favor Peadar, and he has a slight advantage."

"What's that?" Peadar asked, waiting for a reply, but as with leaving, the question was left unanswered.

Kinley closed his eyes waiting for some sign or clear direction from The Crystal Heart. He fingered the leather wrapped shards in his pocket trying to coax an answer out of them, but nothing came. He opened his eyes and slowly turned in a circle, willing something to pop out at him. "Well, what's taking so long? What happened to his advantage?" Peadar asked.

"Just hold on." Kinley said, his tone frustrated and intense.

His eyes scrunched together in concentration as he continued turning. Finally, Arissa tapped his shoulder noticing, when he stopped, that his balance was off. She steadied him as dizziness filled his head. "I think we should just pick a direction and go with it, maybe something will come to you as we walk." she told him.

"Good idea." He said placing his hand on Arissa's shoulder as his head continued to spin. He regained steadied vision just in time to see Peadar roll his eyes through the darkness. "Well?" he asked, "Where do you guys think we should go?"

A little attitude showed on Peadars face, "How should I know, I just found out I was going somewhere."

Tenderness showed in Arissa's eyes as she glanced at Kinley and started walking, following the Endurance River to the northwest.

"I guess we're going that way." Kinley said. He followed Arissa leaving Peadar scowling in his direction. Before too long, Peadar lost sight of Kinley and Arissa, he ran after them to catch up.

*　　*　　*

They walked until their legs couldn't support them anymore, eventually reaching the Endurance River, following it away from the Trading Post. When they got tired, they constructed a rough camp, which consisted of a small fire and a few of the lightweight and ancient cloth mattresses that were stuffed with dried brush. Silence had seemed to take over their journey until this point, and there was a very aggressive and tentative feel in the air.

Kinley pulled the glow-grub bulb from the spot where it hung on his waste, tying a longer cord from the bulb to the loop, so he was able to dangle it into the river.

"I'm going to get some fish, since I'm pretty sure none of us packed any, then we should probably rest up." Peadar glowered at him, obviously still upset about Kinley not knowing where they were headed.

Arissa nodded, "Be careful, we don't need to be carrying you around if you get bitten." she shot him a playful smile, obviously trying to lighten the mood. This made Peadar stare daggers into Kinley.

He walked from where they were set up down to the river, and looked around, having just left the Trading Post they were not yet close enough to see The Mountains of The Crystal Heart in the distance through the darkness.

"Maybe we should start there, it makes sense

that to create a beginning, and we should start at an ending." Kinley spoke aloud, though no one was listening. Kinley lowered the glowing orb into the water; the current swept it past him a little ways.

"Great" he said softly, the edge of the blue light was extending just past his hand and to make matters worse, his glow-grubs were old and near death so their light was weak.

"This is going to make this difficult, must be the Endurance River, it always has the strongest current." he said with a sigh, lying on his stomach at an angle and reaching out towards the bioluminescent bulb. He wiggled his fingers while dragging his hand back and forth in the water to create a commotion. Under the distorted surface of the water, he saw a shape coming up from underneath, it started out as a dark forest green amorphous blob, but as it got closer to the light the color brightened up and so did the shape of the gaping mouth coming towards his hand.

Once he identified the creature coming towards him as the acid green fish that bit him before, he ripped his hand out of the water and leapt to his feet, completely soaking himself in the process. The fish leapt out of the water high enough to expose it from tail to tip, it flipped and rotated in the glow-grub light, splashing back into the water, drenching Kinley a second time. A silence followed as Kinley waited on the bank of the river for the acid green fish to, somehow, sprout legs and chase after him.

It didn't happen and as Kinley waited, he grew tired of standing alone on the riverbank, cold and wet. The glow-grub bulb had snapped open, allowing most of the slow fat creatures to burrow into the newly dampened soil, leaving less than a handful in the bulb.

Kinley plucked a few out of the ground whose tail ends were still exposed, and placed them back into the bulb. The blue-white light was even dimmer than before, and now it throbbed, which reminded Kinley of the light that radiated from the shards of The Crystal Heart.

He looked down at his fingers and wiped the glowing residue that clung to hem on the rough ground. The luminescent streaks throbbed as they faded, leaving nothing behind. He snapped the bulb shut again and dangled it into the water, dragging it back and forth to see if he could lure the acid green fish closer to the surface, but it didn't show up. Instead, he briefly saw a blood red tailfin dark by the light. He was familiar with this fish, and though it was extremely dangerous to catch due to the razor sharp dorsal fin that ran the length of its body and put off a very faint red glow, its meat was sweet to the taste and was so tender that some say it melted away on the tongue.

Kinley's field of vision was extremely limited by the lack of light from the bulb, which was only a quarter of the way full, which meant he needed to think of a new way catch the river beast. He pulled the bulb from the water and tied part of the leather cord, closest to the glow-grub bulb, to his thumb, leaving enough room for the bulb to float to his wrist, illuminating his hand. He plunged his arm into the water up to his shoulder, just barely keeping his face above the water. He wiggled his fingers and watched as the bulb bobbed up and down, almost weightless. His other hand was poised above the surface; a sharpened knife made of stone in is grip, waiting to come down on his prey. He watched as flicks of a fin and glimpses of teeth, and flashes of a bright eye came into and immediately left the lit area. Kinley wiggled his fingers faster waiting for the fish to strike, the muscles in his arm tensed and Kinley was ready to thrust his arm into the water.

In one swift movement, the fish went for Kinley's hand and the knife came down shaving the razor sharp dorsal fin off its body, the water turned black with death. Now that the danger of the fish's dorsal fin had been removed, Kinley grabbed the thrashing creature with both hands and hauled it out of the water, leaving the water dark and frothy. He dropped the fish on the riverbed and brought the knife down, severing its head.

It was now that he was able to get a closer look. A deep green line ran down the side of its body, which gave off a faint green glow, no brighter than the red glow of its dorsal fin. Two long bone spears jutted from its jaw, each side was able to move independently. Teeth shot down and out of its upper lip, leaving the lower bare. Its eyes faced forward and its head came to a sharp point at the top and continued until it would have met with the now absent dorsal fin.

Four sets of dark green pectoral fins tipped with glowing red, ran down the length of its body starting by the head, no bigger than Kinley's thumb, but growing larger and to a more defined point the further back they went. The dark green stripe faded away before it reached the tail, which adopted the blood red color which surrounded the green. Kinley picked up the head of the fish and tossed it into the water, leaving it to feed the other fish that were scavenging along the bottom. Kinley quickly filleted the fish, discarding the rest of the scraps in the water as well. He picked up the fillets and walked back towards the makeshift camp.

When he arrived, Arissa and Peadar were sitting by the fire, looking out into the darkness. A flat stone was already lying on the fire, and a container of the white flecks that Caedmon had given to Peadar was sitting next to the fire. Arissa saw Kinley coming and poked at the fire, trying to arouse some more heat. Kinley laid the fillets onto the hot stone, skin side down and let it sit. Arissa took some of the white flakes and sprinkled some onto the fish.

When the fish was ready to flip, Kinley took a couple of chipped stone poles and slid them under the fish picking it up and flipping it over in one swift motion. A few of the scales stuck to the hot stone. When it was finished, he carefully moved the hot stone off of the fire. He flipped the fish over and noticed that the bright red meat of the fish had dulled to a pale red color. While they were cooking, everyone was silent, but once they started eating the conversation picked up. "I think we should head to The Mountains of The Crystal Heart." Kinley said after swallowing a mouthful of the succulent and sweet fish.

"Why start there?" asked Arissa.

"When I was down by the river I looked around to try and see where we were, there was nothing in view, and I thought of the mountains, then when I went to lure the fish to me, the acid green fish showed up and it just… felt right." he said.

Peadar grunted, obviously not pleased with taking directions from a fish. Arissa looked more afraid for Kinley then pleased with the fact that they had a direction to travel in. Kinley rolled his eyes and silence followed the rest of the meal. When the fish was gone, and the rest packed away, they rolled out their mattresses and went to sleep.

*　　*　　*

Kinley woke up slightly disappointed, grogginess still lingered over him as he realized that the dream he was hoping for hadn't come. Arissa and Peadar were already awake, packed to leave and eating some of the left over fish from before the sleep. He quickly bundled his belongings together and joined them glancing at the near empty glow-grub bulb that hung from his waist.

"Did either of you happen to remember to bring some glow-grub eggs?" he asked as he tossed a piece of the fish into his mouth.

"You didn't?" Peadar asked accusingly, frustration welling up in his tone.

"I didn't really think about it," Kinley said, allowing some stiffness into his voice "did you?"

"Well, no," Peadar replied, he shifted his eyes down to his feet, "but you're the one that's supposed to be the best fisher." the last part was under his breath. Kinley ignored it and looked hopefully at Arissa. She answered with a weak smile and a slight shake of her head. Kinley untied the bulb from his waist and shook it around, swirling the glow-grubs inside, he noticed a few of the small dark translucent eggs at the bottom, but nothing substantial. "We have a few, but we should probably try to find some more soon."

"Well," Arissa said, "we should probably do that before we get too far and actually need them."

Kinley Arissa and Peadar, with bundles on their backs, trekked to the riverbed, searching out any form of rock that could be hiding the dark translucent orbs underneath. Peadar stumbled over to one that took him and Kinley to lift, and as soon as Arissa could see under it she squealed with delight. By the time Kinley and Peadar had flipped the rock over, set it down, and were able to see, there were only a few glow-grubs left, they quickly scooped up the remainders and stared down at the tiny glowing circles where the others had burrowed deep down, blue-white light from the residue already fading. .

Arissa ran to them, handing them each and flat triangular shaped stone, just bigger than Peadars hand. As quickly as each was grasped the person holding it was on their knees scraping at the compacted dirt under the rocks, making their way down to where the fat little grubs felt safety, and to where they lay, atop their eggs, keeping them warm against the moist, cold earth.

Before too long each of them had a pile of dirt between their knees with glowing blue-white particles speckled throughout fading into nothingness. Peadar, the first to start scraping was the first to reach the hollow abyss underground. Light emanated from the tiny hole and Kinley and Arissa set their stones down and started pulling the earth at the edges of the hole into their piles, widening it with every scrape.

Blue-white dirt glowed under their fingernails as they revealed an empty area, alit with glowing dirt walls. At the base of the small cavern was a writhing mass of what seemed like gelatinous ovals, scrunching and squirming this way and that. Between them Kinley could see tiny perfectly round translucent orbs, larger than a grain of sand but smaller than the eye of the fish he catch.

He and Arissa each removed a glow-grub bulb from their waists and started filling them with both eggs and the pudgy little worms. Whatever eggs and worms were left by the time their bulbs were full were scooped up and placed in a basket of dry sand. The glow-grubs instantly dug their way down. Peadar watched as Arissa and Kinley shook their bulbs, trying to separate the eggs from the glow-grubs, and as they shook, the grubs went to the bottom and the eggs to the top. Once they were separated, they poured the eggs into the sand and pushed it around them. They placed the top on the basket and loaded it on the top of Peadars pack.

"I guess we should continue on our way." he said, securing the basket with a few straps and then giving it a tug to make sure that it wouldn't come lose. Peadar hoisted the pack onto his back and the three of them began to walk in the direction of The Mountains of The Crystal Heart.

*　　*　　*

"How much longer until we can rest?" Arissa complained, her footsteps shuffled heavily across the barren ground beneath her feet.

"Not long, I'm a bit tired too, what about you?" Kinley asked, gesturing towards Peadar.

"I could keep going." he said between what seemed like carefully measured breaths. A moment after his comment, Arissa stopped, followed by Kinley.

"Did you hear that?" she asked. Kinley looked around, not to sure what his own reply would be.

Peadar joined them, "What's going on? Why did you stop?"

"Just… Shhhh." Arissa said, she scraped her foot across the ground, as she had been dragging it before. Along with the normal scraping of rock on rock muffled by layers of dirt, there was something else. Something that almost resonated with a ting. At once, all three members of the team dropped to their knees and began sifting through the dirt and rocks, trying to find a texture or material that would make that sound. Peadar pulled his hand to his chest with a surprised grunt. Arissa and Kinley looked to him as they watched a dark trickle of red flow around his wrist. It made its way to his elbow and seemed to pour down to the dirt in a steady stream.

"We've got to get you patched up." Arissa said after the shock of seeing Peadar bleeding had worn off.

Peadar pulled his hand from his chest and stretched it out towards Arissa; his eyes darted off to side for a brief moment as if he was trying not to focus on his wound for long. Arissa grabbed a piece of cloth and wiped the blood away, revealing a quickly healing gash starting at the base of his palm to just under his index finger. Arissa's hand stopped in the middle of wiping the blood away. She looked down and watched as the skin knitted its way back together. She looked up at Kinley and found that he was already looking at her.

"Arissa," Peadar said with a questioning tone in his voice, "how bad is it?"

"It's already healing." she said looking away from Kinley's face to meet Peadars eyes. "You've found another shard of The Crystal Heart." She dropped Peadars hand and went back to looking for the shard, knowing with complete certainty that his hand would heal before too long. Kinley grabbed the dimly illuminated glow-grub bulb with one hand, and the pouch with the other three shards of The Crystal Heart with his other.

The moment the shards were unwrapped there was a faint glowing coming from under the loose dirt that Arissa was searching through. It didn't take much for Arissa to unearth the flat metallic razor sharp chip about half the size of her palm. With how flat the shard was, there was no opacity to it, Arissa picked the shard up, careful to avoid the razor sharp edges. She rested it on her palm and could feel the beat of the heart pulsating and matching up with her own heartbeat.

"It's still hard to believe," Peadars voice trailed off, "that these little rocks are a part of the actual Crystal Heart. I think even most of the people who were around when it was whole, are starting to think of it as a myth."

"It's true," Arissa said with a note of reverence in her voice, "watch this." She grabbed Kinleys hand, the one with the pouch containing the other three shards of The Crystal Heart. She brought the shard that Peadar had found closer to the pouch and as she did, the flat shard on her hand started glowing, from deep within. She brought it closer, the light got brighter, pulled it away, and it dimmed. Kinley never took his eyes off the shard; there was almost a ravenous look on his face. He opened the pouch and Arissa dropped the flat piece into it.

"I think you're going to need a bigger pouch." she observed.

"Yeah… maybe…" Kinley replied only paying half attention to her words.

Peadar looked down at his hand, down at where the blood had spilled onto the dirt, His blood had been soaked up completely, and his hand showed no evidence of the break. "It's like the dirt is thirsty, like the world is craving The Crystal Heart so badly, that it soaks up any part of it that it can get." Arissa nodded shortly in agreement "I've never thought of it like that, but you're right."

"It's going to take a lot more than that to heal this place." Kinley gestured to the darkness around them with the pouch, "more than this too, we have to get going, we can't stop to rest, not yet. This is far too important to me, to everyone. For now though, this seems as good a place to stop and sleep as any." With that, Kinley pulled the pack from his back and started setting up camp. Once everything was set up and the fire was built, it wasn't long before everyone was asleep and each of them were dreaming, but once they woke, only one dream would be remembered.

*   *   *

Kinley was soaring through the darkness, no, not soaring at all, it wasn't by his own choice, nor could he chose the direction, he was following one of the rivers. The Perseverance River, just about to the split, was rushing by him below; he came to the split in the river and was pulled to one side, heading towards Perseverance Pass. It was too dark to see the mountain range of Perseverance Pass in the distance, but he was sure that's where he was being taken.

"Hello." He tried to say, but once he opened

his mouth, his breath and words were immediately taken from him. He looked down into the river below him, and was able to make out dark shapes writhing in the water, a splash here and there, he followed the river behind him to see, in the distance over the horizon, light was approaching. Before he knew it, in one blink of his eyes, the world went from dark and barren to bright. He looked down at the river again to see the water was a clear blue.

There were a mix of the river beasts in the water and different brightly colored fish, though these weren't the same as the ones in his previous dreams. Before his eyes, once again, grass was sprouting and trees were growing and life was returning to the world, and still he was pulled forward. Perseverance Pass was growing in the distance, Kinley blinked his eyes and once again, the world was pitch black. Kinley looked down towards the river again, but this time he was met with a pair of acid green eyes and a fishes silhouette pacing him. The acid green fish soared up and out of the water and came to rest below Kinley, with its fins outstretched and tail still oscillating back and forth, it looked as if the fish were still swimming.

Kinley blinked his eyes again and the world was lit once more. Below him, the fish was changing, its mouth had flattened out and narrowed, the center was coming to a point, and extending. At the same time, a neck had formed and its head was shrinking. The neck extended out and the scales that had covered its body started changing as well, they became feathers, starting at the head and flowing down to its tail. The dorsal fin sucked into its body and the fins on its side extended to form long elegant wings, which began to flap.

Before Kinley could process what was happening, the acid green fish had turned into a beautiful bird, for the most part it had kept the acid green color. The bird now had an orange beak; its head was a vibrant red, with a yellow crest, which faded into a teal color down the neck, right above its wings the teal transitioned into that toxic acid green that Kinley remembered. As the birds wings beat up and down it moved higher up and got closer to Kinley, until he could feel the air the bird was pushing.

Love? He thought, *are you there?* He was met with silence.

The bird twisted its head to look to the side, its long neck and body followed. Kinley found himself pulled in a new direction; He was in the mountains of Perseverance Pass following the pathway south. He looked down to see animals, living and breathing, something he has only seen in dreams before. He and the bird cut and changed directions again. Now headed the way they came, but on the other side of the river. A strange mountain range was visible in the distance. Below Kinley, there was a herd of animals feeding on the grass, trees were sparse here but life wasn't. There were flowers of every color, shape, and size and he was zooming over all of it. He blinked and the bird had been replaced by the fish once more, the plants and animals had been replaced by darkness. The outline of the mountain range was visible up ahead, but only because it was dotted with fires.

The fish slowed, and so did Kinley, he blinked and, though they were still shrouded in darkness, they had gotten considerably closer to the mountains. *What is this place?* He thought to himself, no longer expecting any sort of answer. Kinley squinted to try and see more detail of this glowing outline of a mountain range, he blinked and was even closer than before, he was able to see shapes, obvious movement, and not just from the flames licking the air. Before Kinley knew what was happening, the mountain range was looming in front of him. The silhouettes projected, by firelight, on the wall of the mountain were dancing and growing as they jumped. There was joy in their steps, and that was something that Kinley had never expected to see, something he never assumed the Ree-Kyae were capable of. They were laughing, playing, and eating some sort of meat that Kinley couldn't recognize. These creatures did not fit the picture of the Ree-Kyae that was painted for Kinley throughout his life.

Kinleys body was pulled to another direction, he blinked and it was light out, all the Ree-Kyae were gone, no longer enjoying the succulent white meat, no longer dancing by the fire, what was left was a pile of bones and smoldering remains of the fires. The fish drifted off in another direction, leaving Kinley alone. Kinley blinked and there was a Ree-Kyae right before him, he panicked flailing his arms, trying to push the sharp-toothed creature away from him, but his arms went right through it, the creature didn't notice as Kinley passed through. In front of him now was a hole in a cliff, leading inside the mountain, and beyond that, a passageway.

The walls of the passageway with lined with a bioluminescent moss and sparkled like it was lined with diamonds, occasionally the moss would recede and a hole would appear, in that hole was a gelatinous clear mass, that was alight with bright green flame. Kinley watched one of those indentations as he passed it, out of two holes, one in each side of the indentation, the gelatinous mixture periodically spurted out and landed in the mass that was lit.

The passageway opened into a large cavernous room, filled with Ree-Kyae, it reminded Kinley of an underground version of the Trading Post. There were booths actually carved into the caves rock wall. As Kinley was pulled past he looked at the wares which were being peddled, there were shoes, different forms of clothing, a variety of animals that Kinley didn't even know existed considering how lifeless everything above ground was. There was a large area that was surrounded by a large rock wall, within the confines of that wall were some of the largest insects Kinley had ever seen. They were about twice the size of Kinley from tip to tip; they had short stubby legs, to many to count, which all came to a point. The creature was unbelievably disproportionate, and as long as it was it was almost as wide. It didn't really have a neck; it seemed to Kinley that the head was part of the body. If it weren't for the very large mandibles, protruding from one end, Kinley wouldn't have been able to tell which end was which.

The amount of color that the creature had surprised Kinley. It wasn't necessarily the skin of the creature that was colored, it was the inside, an opalescent sheen seemed to radiate from deep inside the creature, it spread through its entire body and poured its way through the skin. Kinley could see the creatures' internal organs as well, there seemed to be a dull blue light that the creature put out along with the colors, Kinley watched as one of the Ree-Kyae entered the pen where these creatures were held, and expected the creature to snap the Ree-Kyae in half with the powerful mandibles. Instead of the creature having a temper, it lumbered over to the Ree-Kyae and stood next to it. The Ree-Kyae patted it side, almost with affection, and the creature plopped down on the ground next to the Ree-Kyae.

Kinley was pulled past that scene, and out of the large open area into an ornately carved doorway, this hall was lined with smooth stone and there was no moss growing on the wall. The indents in the wall that held the gelatinous fuel were more evenly spaced in this hallway, at the base of the recessed area was a stone bowl carved out of the rock itself Kinley couldn't see any holes spewing the gelatinous goo, but what was in the bowl was bubbling and boiling beneath the bright green flame. Kinley assumed that these bowls were either fed from the bottom or were constantly manually being tended to. The decoration around these were extremely detailed, it looked like a history was being played out around the edges but it wasn't a history that Kinley had ever heard, it was difficult for him to piece together.

It showed one person splitting off into two, in many different forms and panels surrounding the light. At the next bowl, there was another splitting of the two people, this time it was geographically and the two people parted ways. One went to the mountains; the other went to the rivers and eventually came to rest where the Trading Post is now. In the final frame around that flame, the two people started splitting again. At the third there was a very different scene, close ups of two very different populations were etched in, two very different populations in two very different scenes. Kinley was starting to grasp what he was seeing, it must be what the Ree-Kyae believed was the beginning of life, the beginning of civilization. The person that was at the Trading Post must be the first Varian, and the figure that retreated to the mountains, that must be the first Ree-Kyae.

As Kinley passed by the different scenes playing out he saw that the darkness that took over wasn't the work of nature, it was something that the first Ree-Kyae had brought on, originally Arathia had equal time, light and dark, and that this kept everything living in peace. The original Ree-Kyae had taken that, he had torn himself open and spilled his blood; much like the Man-God had done for the Varians, only when he tore himself open a shroud escaped as well bringing darkness over everything. This happened in the illustrations long before the Man-God tore his chest open and placed his heart at the top of the mountains. There were a few panels in between the two events, depicting how the Ree-Kyae lived and thrived during this time. The panels after brought about the events Kinley was already aware of, the Varian history. The final panel, before another ornately carved archway, showed a Varian at the Trading Post, holding something that brought down the mountains.

Kinley passed through the archway that led to what he could only explain as a throne room. A long empty room with half pillars carved directly into the stone walls leading up to a solitary chair. The throne was made completely of bones from what could have been thousands of people. Around the throne, a ditch was cut into the ground, a river of liquid fire flowed, it was fed from behind the throne, Kinley could see a waterfall of the liquid fire. He looked over the throne again, at the highest point was the full skeleton of one person, it was posed to look like it was climbing up the throne and reaching to the sky, in the center of the skull was a hole. Kinleys vision sharpened and he focused on the hole in the skull, as he gazed at it the skull lifted off the skeleton and broke apart revealing something Kinley didn't expect. Twisting in the air, spinning and rising, above the throne was a shard of The Crystal Heart. Kinley reached for it started flailing in the air, trying to make his way towards it but he couldn't, there was a loud screech and he was spun around, face to face with the first Ree-Kyae to acknowledge his presence.

* * *

Kinley woke with a start and a shake; Arissa and Peadar were both watching him.

"Are you alright?" Arissa asked him. The fire had died down a bit; Kinley couldn't tell how long he had been sleeping.

"Yeah, of course I am. Just a bad dream." He wasn't sure if he was going to tell either of them about the dream he had yet, it could be nothing, but with his record, it was more likely that it was something important.

The truth is that Kinley was unsure if he should even be telling them, the history that he saw around the bowls that held the flame was enough to shake any Varian storyteller. As far as Kinley knew, the history of all Arathians was extremely different from what he just dreamed, and the creatures he'd witnessed both the Ree-Kyae and looming beast, were something that he could barely believe existed, and he'd been the one to actually see them.

"Well? Was it a dream from The Crystal Heart,

or was it just a nightmare?" Peadar asked, rolling his eyes.

"I don't know, but to be honest I doubt you'll believe it either way." Kinley replied He decided to let them in on it. He told them, starting at the beginning, about following the Perseverance River, about how every time he blinked his eyes it changed from light to dark and then back again. He told them about seeing the fish and he described how it changed into the bird, explained the colors, the animals and plants on the ground below him. He told them how he was being pulled and how he was unable to control where he was going. He told them what it was like, seeing Perseverance pass in the light, about the mountains. When he got to the mountain range dotted with fires, his voice halted.

"This next part is going to be hard to believe…" Kinley allowed his words to falter; he looked past both Peadar and Arissa, past the fire, and into the darkness behind them.

"Yeah, because everything else we've heard has been so perfectly believable." Peadar whispered sarcastically.

Arissa hushed him, "This is always where the good parts come in."

"I was coming up to a mountain, as I said before, there was light all over it, fires. I could see movement, but I wasn't sure what it was. I blinked and I was almost there, I blinked again and I was right at the mountain. The movement, it was the Ree-Kyae. They were dancing, eating, talking, and singing."

"What?!" Peadar interrupted, "What are you even talking about; they're not smart enough for that, they're barely above animals."

"Barely above animals is what we thought, but there is more, there were a lot of them, all in one place. There is even more than that though. After I had seen them, and went through them, I went inside the mountain. There was an opening in the side of it, I was being pulled still inside." He explained to them about the cave walls, the moss, the green fires and gelatinous mass that kept them alive. He got to the Trading Post area and explained about the animal, which was something else that was hard for them to believe.

"I tell you, it was there and the Ree-Kyae was actually caring for the thing." He was as surprised saying it as they were hearing it.

"Do you know what this means?" Arissa asked with excitement in her voice.

"That you being happy about this means you're crazy?" Peadar asked, only half teasing.

"No, you moron. It means that if this thing exists, and the other animals that were being sold there, be it for food, pets, whatever. It means there is still life out there, who knows what we'll find." she answered.

"Yup, that, and that you're crazy. You're both crazy; go ahead continue on with your crazy dream." Peadar rolled his eyes.

Kinley continued with his story explaining each of the panels on the walls in the smooth hallway, and the throne room.

"Does that mean, that skeleton with the skull, does that mean it's your father?" Arissa inquired.

"Could be, I guess. Doesn't really make much of a difference to me, point is there is a shard there; a piece of The Crystal Heart is in the throne of the Ree-Kyae king. You do know what that means don't you?"

"You better not say what I think you're going to say." Peadar.

"It means..." Kinley started, but he was interrupted by Arissa.

"We're going to have to go there, we're going to have to go in to the Ree-Kyae Kingdom and get it."

"Why do you sound so excited about this, you are absolutely, completely crazy." Peadar observed, but Arissa had already stood up and grabbed her weapon.

"We are going to have to go there, yes," Kinley said "but we aren't going there right now. We know there is a shard there, but at this point, what we're going to need to do is collect all the other pieces first, make that our last stop, just in case we don't make it out."

"But if we don't make it out of there, it means that they're going to have all the shards, then what'll they do, lock it up so that it will never be assembled again, toss it somewhere it won't be able to be recovered, like in that fire river you were talking about?"

"We're going to have to deal with that when we get to it, we can't just give up now knowing where we have to go, there are a lot more shards of The Crystal Heart out there. We have to gather those before we figure out what we're going to do about the last piece."

"Fine, but what about the animals, like Arissa said who knows what we are going to find out exists out there. This is already a dangerous place, just given what we know, and now we've come to find out that there is a lot more out there than we thought... we can't just..."

"Oh, shut it Peadar. You worry to damn much.

We have to take it a step at a time, got it." Arissa said not wanting to argue any further, "We'll overcome whatever obstacle we have to, with a field of carcasses behind us, if need be."

Peadar dropped his argument, knowing that he'd been beaten into submission. Kinley couldn't help but poke the fresh wound in his pride, "For such a big, strong guy you sure give up quickly."

"Well, would you rather I keep pressing it?" he replied curtly.

"Nope, absolutely not." Kinley couldn't help but crack a smile; it was about time Peadar did just that, since they had started their journey, he had been against everything, questioning every decision. Now, it was time to move on. "Did you guys get enough rest?"

He had already gotten to his feet and moved towards the glowing coals that remained of the fire dotted mountain range, kicking dirt over it to snuff the remaining light and heat out. He didn't get an answer; instead, he was met with Arissa energetically hoping to the area she was sleeping, rolling up her mattress and packing up, and Peadar, begrudgingly doing the same. Once everything was packed and they had hoisted their various supplies onto their backs they continued on their way to The Mountain of The Crystal Heart. Kinley, sure now more than ever, that he would find something there that would change the world.

COMING SOON

Want more out of
your experience?
Take it online!

Find out
about:

Mr. Fix-it

NO VAMPIRES
WEREWOLVES
ONLY THE
REE-KYAE

- ♦ Upcoming books in this series!

- ♦ Upcoming projects that you could be selected to help bring to life!

- ♦ Get your copy of this books signed by the author!

- ♦ Get cool merchandise related to The Crystal Heart!

www.ArcticFlamePublications.com